ABBERTON HOUSE

DEBBIE IOANNA

www.bloodhoundbooks.com

Print ISBN 978-1-5040-7028-7

To my daughter, never hold yourself back because you think what you want is out of reach. Just go for it. Take the risk. It may be the best thing you ever do. And remember... be kind, be brave, be crazy.

Do you believe in ghosts...?

PROLOGUE

February 1916

The house stood on an old, retired farm in a small village near Skipton, North Yorkshire. It had been built in the mid-nineteenth century by a young man called Robert Abberton, whose family had owned the land for many generations. The bricks were multihued, like a beautiful mosaic painting. The large blue wooden door took centre stage on the front of the rectangular house. There were windows on either side with matching blue frames and wooden shutters. On the first floor were several more windows and standing tall on both sides of the roof were large chimneys. It was a great design for its day, admired by everyone. Especially on the inside with its grand staircase and modern indoor facilities. The large rooms were designed for a large family and Robert hoped to fill them with children of his own, with enough boys to help him on the farm.

The farm thrived; however, the same could not be said for Robert's young family. The harsh northern winters took their toll, with his wife dying young from pneumonia leaving him to raise their only child alone. Robert never remarried. When his son Joshua was old enough, he married a local girl called Mary and together they had a child: Elizabeth. With no sons to inherit the land, it and the house were passed on to Elizabeth and her husband Henry in 1914, once both her parents had died, although the farm was no longer running.

By then she was in her late twenties, and had given birth to three children. Mary was the oldest at ten. She was very mature for her age and loved to help her mother out with the housework and looking after the two younger children. With her long dark hair, rounded face and green eyes she resembled her mother. Charlotte was seven but not as keen to assist with the cleaning as her older sister. She was very mischievous, not necessarily naughty, but definitely cheeky, and was loved by all who met her. She had the look of her father: brown eyes and curly fair hair. The youngest member of the family, at just two, was Toby. He was very curious and followed Charlotte around, watching her get into trouble, usually trying to mimic her actions. He didn't speak much, only managing to mutter one syllable at a time.

As the farm was no longer in use it left the family with a lot of land. Some of the fields were rented out to neighbours, which gave them some extra income, and some were kept as a place for the children to explore and enjoy. Elizabeth had a patch for vegetables to grow and a coop to keep a few chickens.

Elizabeth's husband Henry was a very handsome man. He was a doctor, which was not a bad profession for someone so young and from a working-class background. He had excelled in school and was supported at university by a wealthy, aristocratic family he had grown up with while his parents worked in service for them. This was not the kind of opportunity experienced by many people, but this particular lord and lady had no sons of their own to watch succeed in life, so they decided to help Henry and give him the opportunity they felt he deserved. He would never forget their kindness. Now a doctor in a small but thriving village and with a healthy and content family around him he could not have been happier.

Henry was popular in the village. He was a kind man, known and loved by all. He would see his patients as and when he was needed. The elderly Mrs Fincham would call on him first thing in the morning, little Charlie's chicken pox would be seen to in the afternoon, old Gerome's gout in the evening (which was painful after a long day at work in the fields) and then he would help deliver Alice's second baby in the early hours, as it could not wait until the sun came up. After three long hours of labour, baby Edward was born, and Henry would walk home, reaching the door just minutes before the sun made an appearance. He'd get a few hours' sleep before Mrs Fincham would be back with another ailment.

When the war with Germany began, he did all he could as a doctor helping the young volunteers prepare, but eventually his need to do fulfil his own duty came and in November 1915 he left his home and was sent for training to join the army. It was the first time he had been away from his family. In February 1916, after a short visit home, he left for France. As a doctor, he would not be placed in the infantry so would be safe from danger, or at least this was what he told his worrying family. He would have no chance of a visit home until the summer at least. It would be a long six months.

~

December 2015

It had been Catherine's dream to live in a large, old farmhouse out in the Yorkshire countryside for as long as she could remember. She had always lived in new, modern apartments in a busy and loud town centre where there was never any peace from neighbours (above and below) and the constant noise of traffic. She could not begin to imagine how nice it would be to wake up to the sound of birds chirping, to the sunrise rather than the sound of bin lorries and bottle bin collections. In fact, the only birds to be found in the town centre were pigeons, and there was nothing beautiful or harmonious about them.

A small town-centre apartment was not an ideal environment to raise her daughter. Isabella was now five and had a very big imagination. When woken up by the sound of the new upstairs neighbours' cries of passion, Bella had had no doubt as to what could have caused such loud screaming. The spider that her daddy had killed the day before had come back as a ghost to haunt the building and had spent the night terrorising upstairs. She'd hoped it would come to her room the next night.

Nothing scared Bella. This made things easier for Catherine who was often alone while her husband worked through the night. He was a fire fighter and his long, varying shifts kept him away, but he would then have several days at home to spend time with them, although this was not always as relaxing as it sounded. Catherine worked from home. She had set up her own business, baking and decorating cakes for birthdays, weddings and all occasions. She was getting a lot more clients, so money was coming in nicely; however, it usually meant that the kitchen was piled high with cakes and icing and cake boards. Another reason to seek larger and alternative accommodation.

There was no need to look for somewhere close to town. Catherine had most of her supplies delivered and Adam did not mind a long drive to work. He was able to sleep at the station if necessary, so was happy to find a house out in the countryside as Catherine wanted.

Abberton House was perfect and just what they were after. The kitchen was big with room for a dining table, so the spare room behind it could be Catherine's workspace. The lounge was large with an old open fireplace, and a conservatory had been added on to the back in recent years. There were three bedrooms upstairs, room for another baby which they both wanted but had put off due to lack of space in the apartment. The garden was the size of a football field. A lot of the land had been sold off by the previous owners, but they had kept back a generous amount. Adam was particularly looking forward to building a barbeque and spending his summers out in the fresh air, maybe putting together a play area with swings and a slide for Bella.

The house had been empty for several years but was in surprisingly good condition. All that was needed was modernising and decorating. Adam knew that his wife would already have plenty of ideas, before they even put in an offer. He was expecting a battle with the sellers who would likely want a price as close to the house's value as possible, something that he and Catherine, with this their first mortgage, wanted to keep as low as they could. However, the sellers called back within the hour to accept their offer. Adam and Catherine were over the moon. After renting for so long and putting away as much money as possible, they would finally own their own home.

Two months after the offer was accepted, they moved in.

CHAPTER 1

February 2016

It was a cold and wet Friday morning when Adam and Catherine got the keys to their new house. This was not a good omen, according to their elderly neighbour back at the flat. 'The first day is rain, the last is pain,' she had said when they'd returned to pack their belongings. She was always full of superstition, so they knew not to pay any attention. The rain did not hinder them filling the two rented vans with their belongings and setting off to their new home. Bella was in school and was spending the night with her grandparents, so Adam and Catherine would not need to worry about her during the move.

At eleven o'clock they arrived at their new house. Adam had driven the first van, while Catherine drove their car. The second was driven by two of Adam's colleagues, Martin and Paul. They had to be back at the station in the afternoon but were staying long enough to help unload the heavy items. Adam had managed to secure a few days' leave so he would have plenty of time to move in and make their new home comfortable. They started with the furniture. Their sofa looked tiny in the large living room, barely filling a corner. It would mean a shopping trip for a new suite. The kitchen looked very empty as they didn't have a dining table yet; they used to eat from the breakfast counter in the flat since there was no room for anything else. Catherine made sure that all her baking equipment was moved to her new workspace and the beds were set up so they would have somewhere to sleep. After all the day's work they would definitely be ready for a long rest later.

It took most of the day, but they were finally in. Martin and Paul left with the promise of a crate of beer each as thanks for giving up their free time. There was still a lot to unpack, not to mention the long list of companies and utilities that needed to be notified of the move. By six o'clock it was almost dark. The rain was finally easing off. They decided that enough was enough and it was time to eat. Knowing they wouldn't have time to cook something for themselves, Adam's mother had given them a homemade lasagne which just needed heating up in the oven for twenty minutes. It was a blessing as they were both starving.

'I'll get the lasagne sorted,' Catherine said. 'You go set up the TV and DVD player and we'll just watch a movie. I'll ring Sky tomorrow to come and set us up.'

'Will do.' Adam yawned. There was a knock at the door. 'Hang on, I'll get that first. Maybe it's a new neighbour offering us some apple pie,' he said in a badly attempted American accent.

Catherine laughed. She left him to it and set about trying to understand the new oven. It was very large, much bigger and better than the electric cooker she'd had at the flat. There were two ovens, six hobs and a separate grill. This would be amazing for her baking. She could get so much done and the business would grow in no time. She found the right setting and then put the lasagne on the shelf and set the timer. When she looked up and out the window, she saw an old man standing in the garden.

She could only just make out his wrinkled face staring at his surroundings, confused. He held what looked like a tissue across his chest, rustling it with his shaking hands. He wore brown trousers and a long grey cardigan, which had holes here and there. She noticed he was wearing slippers. *He must be frozen*, she thought.

Catherine went to fetch Adam but he was already making his way back into the kitchen.

'Well, that was odd.' He rubbed his chin. 'It was an old man. He was looking for his wife. He didn't seem to hear me. He just kept asking where she was, said she vanished with the children and then he walked away. I didn't know what to do.'

'I think we should call the police. I saw him stood in the garden; he'll get pneumonia if we leave him out there all night.'

'In the garden, you say? Where was he? I'll try coaxing him inside and then sit him in front of the fire to keep warm.' Adam reached for his coat.

'He's just out there.' Catherine pointed to the window, but the man was no longer there. 'Oh, he's gone!' She went to the other window to look further around the back of the garden but he wasn't there either. 'Go look for him before it gets darker. I'll call the police and see if there's been any reports of a missing person.'

Adam went out to look for him and Catherine phoned the police. She gave a description and they promised to come out to search the land to find him. There hadn't been any reports of a missing person, but they would check with the local residential homes to see if anyone had snuck out of their rooms unnoticed. However, they told her the nearest home was three miles away, so the old man would have had a long walk if that's where he came from.

Adam returned after fifteen minutes, wet and cold from the rain.

'I couldn't find him.' He put his coat near the fire to dry. 'He can't have gotten that far but there were no signs of him anywhere. What did the police say?'

Catherine relayed the conversation.

'Well, if any of the homes are missing a resident there'll be an uproar, so they'll be out searching,' Adam said. 'And if a little old lady has lost her husband I'm sure she'll be on to the police in no time. He seemed really confused. He might have dementia or something.'

'Yeah, I suppose we'll just have to keep an eye out. We don't have any curtains yet, so it won't be hard. If he does come back we'll just have to get him inside and phone the police again.'

Catherine wandered back into the kitchen. She opened the oven and the smell of lasagne filled the air. She'd forgotten how hungry she was. Adam searched through all the cupboards for the plates, finally finding two, and Catherine loaded them up with food. Adam's mother was a great cook and they couldn't wait to tuck in.

Later on, when their bellies were full and they were nodding off on the couch, there was another knock on the door. When Adam looked out he noticed the police car.

'Hello, officer,' he said. 'Is everything okay?'

'You called earlier about an elderly gentleman on the property?' the young officer asked, removing his hat.

'Yes, we did,' Adam said as Catherine appeared at his side. 'Have you found him?'

'Unfortunately not,' he responded. 'None of the homes are missing anyone and no one else has reported a missing person. We've had officers out searching your garden – sorry if we've disturbed you – and the surrounding area but we've not seen him. I just thought you'd like to know, and if you do see him again please call me directly on this number.' He handed them a card with his name, PC James Shackleton. 'Try and bring him inside if you can, keep him distracted and warm until we get to him.'

'We will do. Thank you for letting us know,' Catherine said, taking the card.

'Not at all.' He returned his hat to his head and set to leave. 'Have a good night.'

He walked down the garden path and Adam shut and locked the door. He yawned and stretched, and Catherine wrapped her arms around his front. They stood for a few moments enjoying the peace, not only from their surroundings but also from being child free for the night. It was a novelty and an opportunity they weren't going to waste.

'Time for bed?' asked Adam.

'Mmm, definitely.'

CHAPTER 2

'*A*re you ready for the new house, Bella?' Catherine turned around in the passenger seat of the car to look at Bella, who sat behind the driver's seat.

'Yeah, Mummy. Grandma said my room will be lots bigger.'

'She's right! You will have loads of room to play now. Lots more space than before.'

'I can't wait!'

They drove through the busy, bustling town of Keighley; the loud noises of squawking children being ignored by their parents on the paths and drivers honking their horns drowned out the car radio, and the smell of exhaust fumes and takeaways filled their car.

Once they were into the countryside the noise faded and the air smelled fresh. It was noon but there was still a presence of frost which made the air nice and crisp. They were soon on the lane to their new house which Bella would be seeing for the first time.

'Here we are,' Catherine said as they pulled to a stop. 'Oh, hang on, don't go yet.' Bella was already trying to free herself of her seat belt. 'Daddy will help you out.'

'I want to see, I want to see!' she screeched. 'I want to see my big room!'

'I want never gets,' Adam piped in. He used his scolding tone but winked at her from the rear-view mirror.

Bella blushed as she smiled back at him, now waiting patiently for her door to be opened. She was never naughty and almost never got told off, but she could occasionally get overexcited.

'Here we go then.' Adam opened her door and helped her jump out. Catherine unlocked the front door and they let Bella walk in first. It was the biggest house she had ever seen, but she didn't show any apprehension before entering. She ran straight into the hallway and up the stairs in front of her. She went in and out of every room, her heavy steps reverberating loudly on the ceilings in the rooms downstairs. They would certainly know where she was when she was playing hide and seek.

'Wow!' They heard Bella cry out. 'My bedroom!' Catherine and Adam reached her room and found Bella lying on the floor like a starfish. 'Look at all my room! I can play properly now.'

'Yes you can,' Catherine said. 'And now Daddy can build up all those toys that Santa brought you for Christmas.'

'Not until he's had a cup of coffee,' Adam responded. 'Are you going to stay up here Bella so Mummy and me can go downstairs for a drink?'

Bella didn't reply. She was too distracted by her room, so he and Catherine made their way downstairs. They each stood in the kitchen with their cups of coffee going over what new furniture they needed to buy and when they would have chance to get to IKEA and other shops to have a browse. They didn't have the internet set up yet so couldn't look online. They could hear Bella running around in her room. The sound moved to the landing, to the bathroom, the spare room and finally their own bedroom. They left her to explore and took themselves to the living room to sit down. She'd be down in no time. The noise had returned to

Bella's room above where they were sitting, quietly listening to her.

'What on earth is she doing?' Adam asked. 'It sounds like she's training for the marathon! She can't be doing this if I'm trying to sleep through the day. I have some night shifts coming up soon.'

'I'll go see. She's overexcited, but she'll calm down once she's settled in. We could always get some rugs to cover the hardwood floors. I'll add them to the list.'

Catherine made her way upstairs, careful not to make too much noise herself. It was cold on the landing and reminded her that they would need to figure out the central heating. When she got to Bella's room, she was surprised to find her fast asleep on her bed. She called her name but there was no response. She must have tired herself out, Catherine thought. She walked over to the bed and placed a blanket over her. Bella always looked so peaceful when she slept. She had fallen asleep in a funny position with her hand placed awkwardly under her face. Something in the doorway caught Catherine's eye, a flicker of movement. There was nothing there when she looked up.

'She was fast asleep on the bed when I got there,' she told Adam as she re-joined him in the living room. 'All that running around must have tired her out. That or she stayed up with your mum all night. I bet she won't sleep tonight now.'

'She'll be fine, she'll sleep. I'll take her for a long walk around the garden later, that'll definitely tire her out.'

There was a bang from the room above and then the sound of little feet running up and down the landing.

'Bella?' Adam called out. 'What are you doing, love?' He turned to Catherine who had started to make her way back upstairs. 'That was a quick nap.' He left her to it and switched on the laptop, forgetting for a moment that they wouldn't have wifi for a few weeks. He'd have to wait until he got back to the station in a couple of days. He closed it back down and pulled out his phone. The signal was weak, but he might be able to connect to the internet this way to check his emails and Facebook. Catherine reappeared a moment later. 'What's wrong?' he asked, seeing the confused look on her face.

'She's still asleep, in the exact same position under the blanket where I left her. She hasn't moved. And I found this outside her room. It wasn't there when I left or I would have fallen over it.' She held out one of Bella's teddy bears. Catherine didn't remember unpacking this one yet. How did it get on the landing?

'Bella probably grabbed it whilst making all that noise, heard me shout up and then jumped back in bed. You know what she's like. She'll be messing about.' The noise upstairs started again. 'Leave her to it for now. In any case I won't need to run her around the garden later to tire her out.'

Adam's reasoning made sense, but Catherine was certain that Bella hadn't moved even an inch. How could she get back into exactly the same position so quickly, with her left hand under her face, little finger on her lip pulling her mouth slightly open?

A little after two o'clock, Bella appeared in the kitchen where her mum was unpacking all the pots and pans. Catherine wasn't used to having so much space. Back in their flat, pans were all piled on top of each other, crammed into a small space, but here they could spread out.

'Mummy, I'm thirsty.'

'Okay, darling. Would you like some water or milk? Daddy has gone shopping so will be bringing home some juice for you.'

'Can I have milk, please?'

Catherine got the milk from the fridge and poured some into a small glass, adding one of Bella's favourite treats.

'Here you go, darling. I mixed some chocolate powder in it for you.' She handed the drink to Bella, who started gulping it down, almost spilling it on her top. 'You were being very noisy upstairs after I left you. Did you decide on more running around, exploring?'

'What, Mummy?' Bella stopped drinking. Catherine raised an eyebrow at her before responding. Bella understood and rephrased. 'Pardon, Mummy?'

'Much better.' Bella occasionally forgot her manners so Catherine liked to remind her. 'You'd fallen asleep so I put the blanket on you, but then we heard you running around again. It makes a lot of noise, you know, so maybe we should have a house rule: no shoes in the bedroom, okay?' Catherine wasn't mad, there was no need to be, but Bella looked back at her mum with a bemused expression.

'Mummy, I've been asleep. I only woke up now and came down for a drink. I haven't been running again, I promise.' She looked to the table and saw her teddy. 'Barney! Yay! I've been waiting for you to unpack him for me.'

She picked up the teddy and walked back to her room, leaving her shoes at the bottom of the stairs.

CHAPTER 3

'*H*ow long will it take you to get to work?'

'About an hour if traffic isn't too bad.' Adam was putting his uniform and some food into his rucksack for work. 'Will you be okay?'

It was Sunday morning and Adam's first day back at work since the move. Now he was faced with leaving his family alone in the new house, he was feeling anxious. It had only just dawned on him that they were no longer living in a highly populated area. They were quite alone out here.

'We'll be fine, it's no different to being alone at the flat. Bella will be in bed early to prepare for her first day at the new school tomorrow. I have lots to do and I'm expecting a call from a couple enquiring about a wedding cake later, so don't worry.'

'Okay.' Adam picked up the car keys and gave his wife a kiss. 'I should be home just after ten tonight if nothing major happens. Call me if you need me.'

'I will, I will, now go or you'll be late.'

Catherine watched her husband walk to the car and then drive out of sight. She made sure the door was locked knowing that Adam would not be happy if she'd left it open for anyone to walk in. She knew there was less risk of danger here than when they lived at the flat, but she didn't want him to worry about her when he was supposed to be focusing on work. She hadn't been completely honest with him though. She wouldn't be okay, but only because she still hadn't figured out how the central heating worked. The radiators would come on, but after half an hour they would switch off again. She kept the fire on in the living room and made Bella bring her toys downstairs where it was warm.

'Bella?'

'Yes, Mummy?'

'I'm going into the back room to do some work. Let me know when you get hungry and we'll make some lunch, okay?'

'Yes, Mummy.' She carried on playing with her farm animal set, talking to each individual animal and to an imaginary friend. 'You look after the horses and I will look after the pigs. Yeah, like that!' Catherine felt sorry for her when she did that. She couldn't wait for her to make some school friends so she could talk to some real children instead of made-up ones. Catherine would make sure to speak to some of the other mums to arrange a play date some time.

She took herself to her new workspace and set about looking through the paperwork from the solicitor in search of instructions on the heating. There were various kinds of documents, some dating back to when the house was built: deeds, tenancy agreements from land being leased, solicitor's documents from land being sold, building regulations for the construction of the conservatory, instructions for the oven, decades-old newspaper articles and many other things, but nothing relating to the heating. She would have to mention it to Adam when he got home. Spring was coming but it was still bitterly cold during the night.

Catherine kept herself busy through the rest of the morning. She received a phone call from her sister in London, made lunch for her and Bella, then had another a phone call from the new clients to set a date for them to have a meeting at the house the following week. It was mid-afternoon when she decided it was time for a break and a sit down in the warm living room with her daughter. Whilst she was in the kitchen, Bella came running in.

'Mummy, there's a man in the window.'

'Excuse me?'

'A man, Mummy, an old man. He keeps walking around the garden and then looking in the window.'

Catherine knew straight away who it was. How could he still be lost? Maybe Adam was right and he did have dementia and this would be a frequent occurrence. When she glanced out of the kitchen window she saw him walking back down the garden away from the house. He was wearing the same old clothes.

'You wait here, Bella, okay? Mummy needs to speak to him. Stay here,' she instructed her daughter whilst quickly putting on her coat. She unlocked the door and ran down the path towards the old man.

'Excuse me? Sir? Can you hear me? You need to come inside, it's too cold out here.' He couldn't hear her. He kept on walking ahead of her looking all over, left to right, as though searching for something.

'Mister? Oh–' Just as she was about to reach him she tripped over a root and landed on her knees. Adam would need to deal with that root. It was one thing having a lost old man wandering around the garden but it would be really bad if he got injured in the process. 'Bloody hell,' she muttered. There was a small hole in her jeans from the fall. She looked up and the man had vanished. Where had he gone? He was barely walking one mile an hour. She looked all around but couldn't see him anywhere. How could he have vanished so quickly?

A shiver went down Catherine's spine, and not just because of the cold wind around her. She looked back at the house and Bella was standing in the doorway holding Barney and staring at her mum.

'Did you see where he went?' Catherine asked Bella, hoping she would shed some light on the situation.

'He disappeared.'

'Yes I know that, but where to?'

'No. He disappeared, he vanished.'

'People don't just vanish, Bella.' They walked inside and shut the door. 'He must have walked or run somewhere? Did you see?'

Bella shook her head.

Catherine locked the door after one final glance outside, wondering how he could disappear so quickly.

CHAPTER 4

March 1916

*E*lizabeth and the children were starting to adjust to life without Henry, although they prayed for his safety and anxiously awaited his letters. There was always one for the children and a separate one for his wife. Henry promised to write to his family every week, and they would reply in return to keep him up to date with news and events from home. Elizabeth tried to write to him most days when she could. She knew he wouldn't get them all individually and that it would mean some days he received two or three of her letters but that didn't matter. As long as they were in regular contact, all would be okay.

My dearest children,

This is certainly an adventure I am on here. It is very noisy. At night I play cards with some of the other men and see to the patients when needed. I have been eating lots of biscuits, a new kind that we don't have at home. As soon as I can return I will make sure to bring some with me for you all to try. Make sure to help your mother around the house and with the chickens too. Don't leave her to do everything on her own.

I love you all,

Daddy.

My dearest wife,

The nights here are very cold. I long to sit with you in front of the fire again soon. I am counting down the days until I can come home and be with you.

I received your first three letters together, and then two more a few days later. It was wonderful to read them. Please keep them coming.

I have been treating a gentleman who lives nearby us at home by the name of Michael Staines. He will be travelling home soon as he has had his left leg amputated below the knee. He is only twenty-one years old, can you believe it? He lives with his dad, Arthur. His mother, Anne Marie, died when he was young. I've told him that he must visit you for his clothes to be mended. I hope that's okay. He is in a poor state. I worry that he won't get the right care at home and I think he needs some company. I don't think his dad will be much help from what I have heard. Michael is a lovely young boy. Once he adjusts to how things are I think he would be handy to have around. I would feel better knowing there was someone to watch over things while I am away. He is looking forward to meeting you and the children.

Write soon my love.

Yours,

Henry.

My dearest Henry,

It is such a relief to hear from you. Your letters arrived only minutes ago and I couldn't help but write my reply straight away. I will save the children's letter until after their tea later. It will be a nice surprise for them.

Of course I will help Michael. My father used to speak about his mother when I was younger and I remember when she died. I didn't *know they had a son. I will keep him busy and distracted and I'm sure he will help us in return.*

You'll be pleased to know I have started to make some money from my sewing skills. After I repaired the vicar's clothes last month he recommended me to some of his parishioners. It's not a lot of money but it is coming in useful.

The children have been very helpful. Mary looks after Toby while I work, and I've been teaching Charlotte how to wash and mend clothes. She is really maturing although she still teases Toby and chases him around the house. All I seem to hear is their feet banging about upstairs. As soon as you return we should look into getting a carpet on the landing.

Write to me again soon.

Yours,

Liz.

When Elizabeth first set eyes on Michael she wondered how he'd survived the war at all. He was taller than she was but he was very skinny, his clothes hanging off him. She invited him inside and immediately started to heat up soup for him to have with some bread. He looked like he'd not eaten for days. He stood shyly in the kitchen corner with one hand holding his flat cap to his chest and the other holding a walking stick. He clearly had a false leg but Elizabeth noticed he was not putting any weight on it at all. *He must be in so much pain*, she thought. She had to hold back tears knowing that her husband could also face the same fate in the trenches.

'Michael, won't you sit down?' She pulled back a chair and gestured for him to come forward. He looked like he would fall over if the wind blew. 'I'm heating some soup for you.'

'Thank you, Mrs Jones. This is very kind of you.' He limped over to the table, wincing with every step.

'Please call me Liz, and ignore the children upstairs, they can be very loud.'

Every bang upstairs startled Michael and it made him more nervous, like he was reliving a traumatic memory. Elizabeth put a bowl of hot soup in front of him with a few slices of bread. He picked up a slice and dipped it in the soup and began to relax a little as he tucked in. It was as though the hot soup was soothing his cold body like a much-needed medicine.

'This is wonderful, Mrs... Liz. This is really good. I've never eaten anything so nice.' He began to get some colour back in his pale cheeks.

'Well, you can have as much as you like, Michael. There is plenty left on the stove, so you just help yourself. I'm going to start to work on your clothes now.' There weren't many, she thought, as she picked up the package of clothes he had brought with him. 'I'll just be in the room to the back of the kitchen, just through there.' She pointed to the door. 'Come get me when you're done.'

Elizabeth worked on fixing his clothes as much as she could; however, some of them looked like they needed to be thrown away. She was tempted to give him some of her husband's old clothes. When she re-entered the kitchen after she'd finished, she saw Michael sitting at the table. His bowl was empty and he was staring at the wall, his lips twitched as though he was muttering to himself and he seemed to be holding back tears.

'Michael?'

This startled him. He immediately jumped up to attention as if back on duty in the army, forgetting that it would cause him such pain in his leg.

'Calm down, it's only me.' She went over to him. 'Have you had enough soup?'

'Yes, Mrs Jones, I mean Liz, I-I'm sorry,' he stuttered.

'Don't be sorry, there's nothing to apologise for. I should be sorry for making you jump. I've finished your clothes.' He took the package of clothes from her and picked up his stick.

'Thank you, Liz, you're very kind.' He made to go towards the door. 'Thank you for the clothes and food. It was very nice of you, but I must go now. Father will be wondering where I am.'

'Of course, come back and see me won't you? I think it would be a good idea.'

'Yes, Liz. Thank you, Liz.' He opened the door, not making eye contact with her. 'Goodbye, Liz.'

When he was gone, she picked up her pencil to write a quick letter to Henry.

My dearest Henry,

I met young Michael today. I am very concerned about him. I mended his clothes, but I asked him to come back and see me soon. He needs some company besides his father. If he is left alone with him all day he is sure to go mad. I might write to the war office and see if there are any local groups he can go to for support. What do you think? If anything, I can feed him. He looks like he hasn't eaten a proper meal in a long time.

I'll do my best to look after him. I hope you're safe.

All my love,

your Liz.

CHAPTER 5

*E*lizabeth had several letters to post to Henry. Each of the girls had written their own notes and she had written two herself. She decided that she would walk the girls to school on this windy Wednesday with Toby so she could call at the post office after. Toby walked happily at her side. Once the girls were inside the school hall, she and Toby continued to the post office which was only a few minutes down the road.

"Ow's 'e getting on?' Mrs Holmes asked as Elizabeth left the post office. Mrs Holmes had lived in her small cottage next door to the post office all her life, eighty years to be exact. She could always be found sitting in a chair outside the front door with a cup of cold tea and cigarettes.

'He's okay, I think. Not had much word from him, but from what he has told me, he's all right.' Elizabeth stood by the gate to talk to her.

'It's an 'orrid business. I mean, Betty's son Arthur wa' killed only last week. An' now look at that 'un there, poor lad.'

Elizabeth looked around and was surprised to see who she was talking about.

'Oh, that's Michael. He was with Henry. Henry treated him after it happened.'

They watched him as he navigated his way on the cobbles with one good leg and a crutch supporting the other. The wind was blowing hard against him but he kept going.

'It'll ruin 'im, that leg. They're ne'er the same again. My brother couldn't live with it. Killed 'is sen, 'e did.'

'I'll go and see if he is okay. I'll see you again soon, Mrs Holmes.' Elizabeth picked up Toby and ran across the road to Michael. 'Michael, hello,' she said as he turned around, surprised to see her. He smiled back.

'Mrs Jones, I mean Liz, hello. Sorry, I didn't see you there.'

'Don't worry about it. How are you?'

'I'm okay. Just wanted to get out of the house for a bit of fresh air. I've been sat in for a few days with nothing to do.'

'And how's your leg? You seem to be doing much better on it. I was watching you from over the road.'

He shuffled uncomfortably on the spot, embarrassed that she had been watching him.

'It's not too bad. Still sore but healing. Thank you. I should go.'

'Oh, okay. Why don't you drop by in a few days? We can have a pot of tea if you like and a chat. Might be nice to have a change of scenery.'

'Really?'

'Of course. I meant it when I said to come by and see me some time.'

'Okay, I will... I'll see you soon.'

She watched him walk away until he was out of sight, worried that he might lose his balance on the cobbles. She looked around to see Mrs Holmes was still watching him too, shaking her head at the poor state he had been left in.

'Ay dear, Toby, what shall we do now?' Toby was sitting comfortably in her arms. He looked up at her.

'Lot,' he said with a finger in his mouth.

'No, Charlotte is in school. You can play with her later. What else can we do?'

'Da.'

'No, we can't see Daddy either. Sadly. Come on, we'll see if we can find some of those ducks before we go home.'

CHAPTER 6

*I*t was Monday morning, almost lunchtime. Toby was asleep upstairs and Elizabeth was wondering what to make them both for lunch. Another letter had just arrived from Henry. He wouldn't have received her last one yet. She sat down in the living room and was about to open it when she heard a faint knock at the front door. At first she thought she was mistaken, as it was so quiet it could have been a mouse tapping at the wall. She decided to check and was glad she did, as when she opened the door, there stood a very timid-looking Michael.

'You said to call around,' he said, as though he needed to justify his visit.

'Of course, come in. It's good to see you again, Michael.' She opened the door fully for him and ushered him into the living room. 'Go through there and make yourself comfortable. I'll bring us a pot of tea and then we can talk.'

He walked into the room and sat in the armchair by the fire. He looked around at his surroundings. The walls were white and the ceilings had several wooden beams going across the full length of the room. There were white net curtains in the windows and several framed photos on the walls. Some were photos of Henry, Elizabeth and the children and a few of older relatives. Michael suddenly shivered with cold and noticed that the fire was getting very low. There was a pile of logs next to his chair so he decided to top it up, worried that it might go out completely. It was still winter and had been frosty that morning. He got down on his knees too quickly without thinking and felt a rush of pain. He could not help calling out as hot flare of agony shot up his leg.

'Oh, Michael, don't worry about the fire.' Elizabeth rushed in to put the tray of tea down on the table. 'I can do that, let me help you up.'

'No,' he said quite sharply. 'Sorry. It's just, I must get used to it. That's what they kept saying. To carry on as though it never happened.'

She stepped back and began to pour out the tea but also to watch him as he reached, painfully, to put the wood into the fire. He managed it and winced as he stood up and sat back down on the chair.

'Is it still hurting? Can I do anything?' she asked.

'It's fine. I need to get used to using it again.'

'It might be too soon for that; you've not been long home.'

'I need to find work soon or I'll have no money. The little amount I have won't last long. My dad doesn't have much.'

Elizabeth couldn't believe what she was hearing. A young man's life had been ruined whilst serving his king and country, yet his job prospects were low and he would have no support. What could he do?

'Look, Michael, I can't offer you any money but whilst Henry is away, I could do with some help around here at times.'

'I don't want to be a burden. I would get in your way.' He picked up his cup of tea.

'You wouldn't at all. There's only so much I can do. I can't get the girls to do everything as they have school through the week.

You would be doing Henry and me a big favour, and then if you need a reference for work I can give you one.'

Michael thought about it whilst drinking his tea. It would get him out of the house and into a routine. He liked Elizabeth. She had been kind to him each time he'd seen her and she was exactly as Henry had described. If he got used to doing manual tasks, then it would give him experience to find a job elsewhere.

'Okay, yes, I think that would be a good idea. When would you like me to come back?'

CHAPTER 7

March 2016

The day had come for Bella's first day at her new school and she was one excited little girl. Most children would find being the new child in class daunting, but Bella had no fear. She couldn't wait to meet her classmates and teacher. Miss Mapleton had spoken with Catherine on the phone the week before to make sure that Bella would still be coming and to tell her that the class were excited to meet her too. Her uniform consisted of a black skirt, white polo top and a red cardigan. Wearing this made her feel very grown-up as there hadn't been a uniform at her previous school. She had some new shoes for the occasion and on the walk to school she was careful to avoid all puddles and mud.

Miss Mapleton was one of those teachers who spent her entire career in the same school and probably taught some of her current pupils' parents when they were the same age. Her white hair was curled on top of her head and her glasses hung from a multicoloured beaded chain around her neck. She wasn't very tall and wore some very old-fashioned clothes, but she was very friendly and welcoming to Catherine and Bella.

'Come in, please come in. Bella, it is lovely to meet you.' She bent down to Bella's height and shook her hand. Catherine was very surprised to see her daughter blush. 'Bella, why don't you take a seat on the carpet with the other children? My helper Miss Arundale is going to do the register so you will be able to hear everyone's names. Why don't you sit there next to Janey and I'll speak to your mum for a few minutes, okay?' Bella sat down next to a little blonde-haired girl who smiled at her, and Miss Mapleton took Catherine to one side.

'Bella will be fine so I don't want you to worry. We're a small class and I have Miss Arundale three days a week. Bella will get a small glass of milk and some fruit in the morning and then lunch around half past twelve. We finish the day around quarter to three but I like to have fifteen minutes of winding down, so either Miss Arundale or I will read a story before we let them out to go home, but feel free to come anytime to collect her. There's an after-school club too, if you're interested?'

It was a lot to take in, but Catherine was very confident that it was a great school. The walls were covered in colourful art by the children and photos of days out and trips. Best of all, Catherine loved Miss Mapleton. She seemed like she would really get to know Bella and spend a lot of time with her. In Bella's last class there were at least thirty pupils but Catherine guessed there were only a dozen in this room. If Bella wanted to stay behind some days for the after-school club that would be fine but for now she wouldn't really need it.

'I'll be here for three o'clock then.' Catherine smiled. She knew that Bella would be friends with the whole class in no time. As she walked out she could hear Miss Arundale asking Bella questions about her last school and what her hobbies were. Bella didn't even notice her mum leaving.

~

This would be the first time that Catherine had been alone in the house for a whole day. Adam was on a long shift and wouldn't be home until midnight, but she had a busy day planned. She had a birthday cake to make for a child's seventh birthday later in the week and wanted to get started on it now as it was due to be collected in the morning. The cake itself was baked and ready but it needed decorating. With the complicated design the mother had chosen Catherine guessed it would take her all day to complete, and it did.

The hours flew by and before she knew it, it was just after two o'clock. The cake was carefully put into boxes ready to be collected the next morning and she put on her coat to go pick up Bella. She thought she had left her keys on the kitchen worktop, but they weren't there when she went to get them. Where had they gone? She searched high and low but couldn't find the keys anywhere. She was completely baffled when she glanced back at the worktop and there they were, exactly where she'd left them. 'I must be cracking up,' she said to herself. She grabbed the keys and walked out the door.

~

'Did you have a good day?' Catherine asked as her daughter ran to her in the playground.

'Yes, Mummy, I loved it. I sat with Janey all day and we played out at playtime on the slide and swings. I was picked to choose the story for Miss Arundale to read before home time. I picked one about a tiger who kept going to someone's house for tea. It was really funny, me and Janey kept laughing.'

'Hello?' A blonde lady approached Catherine. 'You must be Bella's mum?'

'I am, yes.' Catherine noticed the little girl Janey holding on to the woman's hand. 'I'm guessing you're Janey's mum?'

'Ha-ha, yes, I am.' They shook hands. 'I'm Gillian. It's nice to meet you. I've been with Janey for all of seven minutes and she hasn't stopped talking about your Bella.'

'It's nice to meet you too. I'm Catherine. Yes, Bella said she's spent all day with your Janey. I think she's found her new BFF.'

'Definitely. How long have you lived here?'

'Just a couple of weeks. We live over at Abberton House.'

'Oh, really?' Gillian had a look on her face which Catherine struggled to understand. 'And how are you finding it there?'

'It's great, I love it. It's so peaceful, which is a big change to what we're used to. Janey should come over sometime for a play date if you like?'

'Well, yes, sometime, yes that would be good. Or Bella could come to us? We're not far from you.'

'Yes.' Why didn't she want Janey at their house? 'Either way is fine for us, isn't it, Bella? Wouldn't it be nice to see Janey outside of school?'

'Yes, Mummy.'

'There we go. We'll have to get it arranged.'

'Absolutely!' Gillian got her phone out of her pocket. 'Put your number in here and then we can talk to get something organised.'

CHAPTER 8

*C*atherine's sister Emma didn't drive. She didn't need to as she lived and worked in London where everything was a Tube ride away. Anytime she came home to Yorkshire for a visit she would get the train and could always rely on someone from her family to pick her up from the station.

The nearest train station to Abberton House was only a short distance from the village. As it was a surprisingly warm day Catherine had decided to leave the car at home and walk. This way, once she met her sister, she would be able to give her a tour of the village, treat her to lunch and then it would be a nice stroll back to the house. Emma could only stay for one night so she wouldn't have too many bags to carry.

'Emma!' called Catherine. 'Over here!'

'Cat!' She ran to her sister for a hug. Emma looked as glamorous as ever. Catherine had never known anyone else who could look like a *Vogue* cover model after nearly four hours of travelling but Emma always managed it. Her hair was a short dark bob, longer on one side, and it never moved. Despite the breeze it was staying firmly in place. She wore black leggings which showed off her long legs and fabulous figure, maroon ankle boots with grey faux fur collars around the tops, a short maroon jacket to match the boots and the grey crocheted snood that Catherine had made for her three years ago. As much as Emma loved unique clothing she also loved her designer bags. She had a small black Michael Kors bag around her shoulder and was also carrying a Ted Baker overnight bag in her right arm. Catherine's Primark handbag was suddenly feeling very boring and inadequate.

'Aw, Cat, you look amazing. Being a country wife really suits you. How's the business going? I can't wait to see the house. Have you guys all settled in now? How's little Bella and that hunky fireman of yours? The last time I saw him was–'

'Emma,' Catherine had to cut her off to allow her to breathe. They hadn't even left the station yet and already Emma was trying to cover all topics. 'Calm down, there's loads of time to talk. I've left Bella with Adam at home so we can have some girl time and catch up. There's a tea room in the village which serves lovely coffee and cake, so I thought we'd pop there first and then walk back to the house. It's not far. Is that okay?'

'Of course it is!' Emma linked her arm with her sister's to lead the way out. 'Let's go for cake!'

It was a ten-minute walk to the village, but it didn't feel that long at all with the constant conversation. They had only seen each other last Christmas but there was a lot to catch up on. Emma was strutting on the cobbles as though it was a catwalk. She had no problem at all, whereas normal people, like Catherine, had a bit of a struggle to negotiate the uneven ground without tripping at least once. They found the tea room and picked a cosy corner to sit in and were soon tucking in to coffee and cake.

'Does it bother you being in such a big house alone when Adam has to work nights?'

'Not really.' Catherine placed her empty cup down on the table. 'The house makes the odd noise at night but Adam promises me that it's natural for old houses to creak and bang. But sometimes...'

'What?' Emma was intrigued. She loved a cliffhanger.

'Some stuff just seems too...' Catherine wasn't sure what word to use, 'weird and can't be explained logically.'

She went on to explain about the old man from the first day and how she saw him again in the garden but as soon as she went outside to investigate he vanished without a trace.

'Well, that could be anything. He might have dementia and every time his wife pops to the shops he probably goes for a wander and gets himself lost. His wife probably knows his pattern so manages to find him.' Emma's explanation seemed reasonable. 'You remember what Granddad was like with Alzheimer's. If you took your eyes off him for a second he'd disappear to the greenhouse to check his vegetables.' There'd been no vegetables in the greenhouse for twenty years but he always went out to check on them regardless.

Emma was right, Catherine thought to herself, of course she was right. There was nothing sinister about a lost elderly man in the garden. What harm would he cause? But what about the other events?

~

They arrived at the house around 4pm. It was still daylight but the sun was hiding behind some clouds. Emma stood and stared at the house.

'Cat,' she began, putting her hand out to Catherine's arm, 'it. Is. Fabulous. I can't believe how big it is! You'd pay millions for something like this in London. Look at the shutters on the windows, how sweet! It looks so exotic. Oh my God, look at the size of the garden! Is all that yours? Think of the barbeque parties you can have! I am so coming back this summer.'

Adam appeared in the doorway. 'Well, well,' he said and folded his arms across his chest, 'look what the Cat dragged in.'

'Adam, you flatterer, get your arse out here and give me a hug.'

'You can take the girl outta Yorkshire, but you can't take Yorkshire outta the girl.'

They both laughed and hugged. They'd not seen each other since Christmas 2012, as Adam usually had to work over the festive period and Emma couldn't come up very often due to work and other commitments. Once they'd let each other go Bella came out to greet her aunty. She'd not met Emma many times before but that didn't stop her running out to get a cuddle too.

Emma glanced up at the house one last time before walking inside but suddenly stopped to stare straight back up at one of the upstairs windows.

'Are you okay?' Catherine asked.

'Yeah...' She was still staring at the window. 'I thought I saw a face in that window but it's gone now.' She was pointing at Bella's bedroom.

'That's Charlotte.' Bella beamed. 'She's visiting me.' She was so happy at having a friend in her room that she didn't notice the look on her parents' faces.

'You have a friend over?' Adam asked. 'You should have told me if you'd invited someone.' He looked to his confused wife. 'I was downstairs the whole time. I didn't hear the door open.'

'She said she lives here. She comes to see me sometimes. She likes to play games,' Bella said defensively.

'Maybe it was a reflection of a bird flying past or something.' Emma provided yet more logical reasons, sensing she was getting her niece into trouble. 'It was literally a split second and then it was gone. Bella probably has an imaginary friend, bless her. Now, can I have my tour?'

'Yes, yes of course!' Catherine responded, noticing the air getting colder. 'Come on, Adam will take your bag and I'll show you around.'

CHAPTER 9

*E*mma had a good look around the house and loved everything about it. She couldn't help but keep commenting on the size of the rooms. All three bedrooms were huge compared to hers down in London. She had finally been able to afford to rent her own apartment after sharing for so many years but it was so much smaller than this. Her entire living space was the same size as the living room. This felt like a mansion in comparison.

It was getting late. They had all caught up properly over dinner and wine and it was now approaching bedtime.

'Are you sure you don't mind the blow-up bed?' Catherine asked as she was setting it up. 'You can have Bella's bed and she can sleep in here.'

'No, don't be silly! I'll have this bed. Why don't you put it in Bella's room, though, and I can sleep in there with her?'

'Oh, Bella has taken to running up and down the landing some nights. She denies it in the morning but I don't want her keeping you up too much. Plus, if you're in the same room she might not sleep herself.'

41

'Why does she run on the landing?'

'I don't know. We thought it might stop once she got settled in but every now and then it happens and as soon as she hears us getting up she runs back in to bed.'

'Are you sure it's her?' Emma asked whilst unfolding the blankets for the bed.

'What do you mean?'

'Don't you think the house is a bit… spooky?'

'Oh, come on, don't be daft. Not all old houses are haunted, you know.'

'I'm serious,' she lowered her tone, 'can't you feel something?'

'Like… cold? That's the dodgy heating.'

'No, you tart.' She threw a cushion at Catherine. 'You don't feel it? I felt it the second I walked through that front door.'

'No, Emma, whatever "it" is, there's nothing here. Just a few creaks and an overexcited, overly imaginative child.' Catherine was used to her sister being dramatic.

'Okay, whatever you say.'

Catherine bid her sister goodnight and went to check on Bella. She understood what Emma was talking about; she did feel something in the house, but she didn't think it was anything spooky. She was alone most of the time so was getting used to the odd sounds. She opened the door to Bella's room. Bella was fast asleep, her left leg hanging out of the bed while she hugged Barney close to her. When Catherine got to her own room, Adam had his laptop in bed. It was such a relief for them to have the internet again.

'What time is it?' Catherine asked.

'It's just after eleven, definitely time to sleep.' He closed the laptop down. 'Is Emma all settled in?'

'Yeah, she's fine. I think she wanted to sleep in with Bella but I didn't think it'd be a good idea. The last thing Emma needs is a sleepless night before she has to head back to London.'

'Good thinking.' Adam kissed his wife as she got into bed and they snuggled up together to get warm. They soon drifted off into a deep, well-deserved night's sleep.

~

Something startled Catherine awake, something by the bedroom door. When she looked over she could see the door was open and a small silhouette stood on the landing.

'Bella?' she whispered, not wanting to wake Adam. 'What are you doing?'

The figure ran across the landing and down the stairs, banging on every step. Catherine cringed at the noise and looked over to Adam, who was still quietly snoring. She carefully got out of bed so she wouldn't wake him up. She waited until she had closed the bedroom door to put the landing light on. She found Barney on the floor and could hear Bella downstairs giggling loudly and running around. Maybe it was a form of sleepwalking and that's why she could never remember the next day.

'Shit!' Catherine cried out as she bumped into Emma. 'You scared the crap out of me!' she whispered.

'Sorry, sorry. I heard Bella running around and it woke me up. Who's this?' She pointed to the teddy in Catherine's arms.

'Oh, this is Barney, her sleeping companion. She must have dropped him on her way downstairs. She can't sleep without–'

'Is this a private meeting or can anyone join in?' Adam walked over to them on the landing, woken up by their encounter.

'Sorry, love.' There was no need to whisper anymore. 'Bella is on the loose again.' They could hear her giggling downstairs still.

'What on earth could possibly be funny at three in the morning?' Emma asked.

'I'll go get her. You guys go back to sleep.' Adam made his way downstairs.

'We normally leave her to it,' Catherine said, 'but she doesn't usually go downstairs. It's usually just a few laps of the landing and that's it. We'll have to speak to her about it tomorrow.'

They heard a noise from Bella's bedroom, a child's cough. They both froze and looked at each other.

'What was that?' Emma asked.

'Erm, I-I don't know.' Catherine looked down the stairs. Adam hadn't returned with their daughter yet. She had a sinking feeling in her stomach. She knew she had to investigate but something was stopping her feet from moving.

'Come on.' Emma grabbed her arm and they headed towards Bella's room. The door was already slightly ajar. When they pushed it fully open they saw Bella tucked up in bed, leg still hanging out, fast asleep. They stared at her in disbelief.

'She's playing hide-and-seek or something down there, I can't find her anywhere.' Adam had reached the top of the stairs and was walking towards them. 'I put all the lights on but she's hidden somewhere, the little... What's wrong with you two?' he asked, seeing the expressions on Catherine's and Emma's faces. 'What is it?' Catherine stood back so Adam could look into the room. He took a few moments to register that Bella was there. 'Okay, she's in bed,' he whispered.

'Guys, what is going on?' Emma asked. 'What is in this house? What is running about downstairs?'

'Emma, there's nothing in this house. It's an old house there's bound to be noises.'

'Adam, come on, house noises don't giggle and drop teddy bears on the landing and run around downstairs.'

'Let's just go back to bed. It's very late and you guys have plans tomorrow before your train back.' Adam walked back to bed leaving the women on the landing.

'Cat, seriously, all three of us witnessed this. Bella is right. It's not her running around at night, it's something else.'

'Emma, I saw something.' Catherine had waited for Adam to close the bedroom door before speaking.

'What?'

'When I first heard it, I looked at the bedroom door and there was a shadow of a girl in the doorway. I assumed it was Bella, why wouldn't I? And I saw her run, actually run away from the door. That's why I got up. I didn't want her to wake you up too. I thought I could find out once and for all why she runs around like this. But it really isn't her, is it?'

'So, there's a girl ghost? And that's her granddad knocking on your door?'

'He's not a ghost; he's a proper human being. A lost human being.'

'Who also vanishes into thin air?'

Catherine thought about this for a moment. Had she seen a young girl running, or was she just tired? Eyes can play tricks on you when you're tired. But can you hear things when you're tired too? They'd lived in this house for about a month now and been woken by this very thing quite a few times. What was going on?

'Okay, come on, let's just go back to bed and we can talk about it tomorrow.'

'I'm not going back in there on my own. Are you mad?'

'Well, I don't think it would be appropriate for you to top and tail with Adam and me, do you?'

'Mummy?' Bella walked onto the landing rubbing her eyes. 'What are you doing? Why do you have Barney?'

'Nothing, Bella honey. Go back to bed. Here's Barney, he got a little lost.' She handed the teddy back to her daughter.

'Hang on there, Bella, you're coming in with me.'

'Really?' Bella looked from Emma to her mother for approval.

'Fine, but you must go straight to sleep, okay?'

'I will!'

Emma and Bella went into the spare room and climbed onto

the blow-up bed together. Catherine closed their door and started to walk towards her own room, speeding up when she heard a giggle from Bella's empty bedroom. She switched off the landing light and quickly shut her bedroom door.

CHAPTER 10

I *can't sleep. I daren't open my eyes but I can't sleep. Adam is by my side so why am I so scared? I feel like a terrified child making sure that no part of my body is exposed. I am fully under the duvet with it pulled right up to just under my nose so I can breathe. I need to fall asleep soon. This is ridiculous. What am I expecting to see?*

'You're already awake?' Adam rolled over in bed seeing his wife's eyes open. 'It's only half seven. I would have thought you'd be sleeping till noon with last night's events.'

'I've not slept.'

'Why? Don't tell me you're actually spooked by all this?'

'Adam, you were there. You were so convinced by the noises downstairs that you actually went down there expecting to find Bella.'

'Well, I was wrong. I was tired after being back on nights. It doesn't mean there's a bloody ghost in the house.' He pulled Catherine towards him affectionately and snuggled up against her. 'It's nothing, just go back to sleep.'

'I need a coffee. Do you want anything?'

'No, thank you.' He rolled back over. 'I'll try getting a few more hours' kip before I take Bella to my mother's.'

Catherine got out of bed and put her dressing gown on. She wanted to sneak downstairs without waking up her sister or Bella. The sun was up now so the house should be a bit brighter, no need for lights. She hesitantly opened the door, not quite sure what she was expecting to find on the other side. Whilst tiptoeing down the stairs she could hear movement in the kitchen. Her heart started pounding in her chest as her body fought against her taking another step. She finally reached the bottom stair and tried to peer around the doorway. The hand came from nowhere, latching on to her right arm and pulling her downwards making her cry out loud.

'Bella!' she shouted.

'Sorry, Mummy.' Bella jumped back, pulling away from Catherine.

'No, darling, I'm sorry.' She realised it was not Bella's intention to scare her. 'You just made me jump that's all.'

'What's going on?' Emma came out of the kitchen. 'What happened?' Emma looked at her sister's pale face and Bella's teary eyes.

'Nothing. Bella gave me a fright, didn't you?' Catherine reached down to pick her daughter up for a cuddle. 'Why are you two up so early?'

'Well, we couldn't sleep as we were a little cramped in that bed together, so decided to come downstairs for some pancakes, but I can't find any flour.'

'Oh, it's in my room at the back for baking. I'll go get it.'

'No, no. You sit down, I'll get it. Judging by the state of the bags under your eyes you need coffee… and make-up.'

Catherine poured herself a cup of coffee and sat at the table. She was joined by Bella who climbed up on her knees whilst Emma made enough pancakes to feed an army. They didn't speak of what had happened the night before as they didn't want to scare Bella. Instead Emma questioned Bella on how she was finding her new school.

'I like it. It's small. I sit with Janey and she's my best friend.'

'That's nice,' Emma said with a mouthful of pancake, 'and where does Janey live?'

'I don't know.'

'She's not that far from here, it's walking distance,' Catherine interjected. 'I'm trying to arrange a play date with her mum for one weekend.'

~

An hour later, a dazed and confused Adam appeared in the kitchen. He looked very pale.

'Are you okay?' Catherine asked.

'Fine. Just fine. Pancakes?'

'My famous recipe.' Emma jumped up from the table. 'Sit down, I'll bring you some. Do you want a cuppa?'

'Coffee, please.'

He sat down next to Catherine who hadn't taken her eyes off him since he'd walked in. What was wrong with him?

'Bella, have you brushed your teeth yet? That tooth fairy won't come visit you in the new house if you don't keep those teeth clean.'

'I'll do them now, Mummy.'

'Good girl.' Bella left the kitchen and ran up the stairs. Emma joined them at the table bringing Adam his breakfast.

'What's up with your miserable face? I make you pancakes and you can't even crack a smile? How rude.'

He gave a very quiet laugh, almost only a loud exhale of breath, but something wasn't right.

'How long have you been down here?' he asked his wife.

'Erm, since I left you at half seven.'

'You've not been back in the bedroom since?' She shook her head at him in response. 'I must have been dreaming then. Don't worry about it.' He took a large gulp of coffee.

'Adam, tell me what happened,' his wife insisted.

'Nothing happened. All this talk of ghost nonsense has got to my subconscious and made me dream about it, that's all. I'm fine.' He picked up his knife and fork and started to tuck into his pancakes, squeezing some syrup onto them first.

'You sure?' Catherine wasn't convinced but she didn't want to push it any further if he didn't want to talk about it in front of her sister. He nodded. 'Okay, then.'

'So, what do you two have planned today?'

It had started to rain as Adam was getting Bella ready to go out. He was driving over to his mother's house in Bradford for the afternoon, leaving Catherine and Emma alone to catch up properly. Emma would be gone by the time they were back, so they said their goodbyes then. She agreed to come back in the summer as long as they agreed to hold a barbeque party. Emma told Bella that she would miss her favourite niece and would telephone as often as she could. Once Adam and Bella had left and the door was firmly shut…

'So, what the hell was that about last night? You didn't tell me you bought the chuffing *Amityville Horror* house! Seriously, Catherine, that was not normal. I couldn't bloody sleep thinking I would wake up with Casper the friendly ghost floating over me.'

Emma never addressed her sister by her full name unless something had really bothered her.

'Emma, honestly, I have no idea. That has never happened before. I told you about the old man but that's about it. If we've ever heard heavy footsteps up there we've always assumed it was Bella.'

'What did Adam say about it when you went back to bed?'

'He thinks it's a load of rubbish. He doesn't believe in any of that stuff.'

'You know yesterday when Bella said about her friend Charlotte? You don't suppose…?'

'No, not a chance. She has a new imaginary friend every week. That's why I'm pushing for a play date with some of her school friends. I don't want her feeling so lonely that she has to make up people.'

'Did anything else happen last night?'

'Well, I thought I'd been awake all night but I didn't hear you guys coming downstairs so I must have nodded off at some point.'

'I told Bella we had to be super quiet, so I carried her and pretty much tiptoed until we were downstairs.'

'After you shut your bedroom door though, and I walked down the landing back to mine, I heard the giggling again but this time in Bella's room. And this time there is no doubt the bedroom was empty, as she was with you!'

'Did you check it out?'

'Did I f… hell check it out.' Catherine never swore anymore for fear of Bella catching on. 'Would you have gone in there on your own?'

'Maybe not,' Emma admitted.

They spent the rest of the afternoon sitting in the living room drinking tea and catching up. Emma updated her sister on work and what it was like to finally be living in her own apartment, no longer sharing. Catherine told Emma how her cake business was now thriving due to her new larger workspace and her new clients coming through weekly. All too soon it was time to walk down to the train station. The rain had stopped and the sun was peeking through the clouds.

'Do you think you'll get another car now you're living way out here?'

'I think so. It's not too bad as I can still walk Bella to school but I'm a bit limited with public transport for visiting anyone. And it makes things awkward if a client wants a cake delivering to them.'

Emma's train was in the station already with just minutes until it was due to set off.

'Thank you so much for coming to see us. Text me when you get home, won't you?' Catherine said, hugging her sister.

'I will, it shouldn't be too late.' She pulled away from the hug and picked up her bag. 'Love you, Cat.'

'Love you too, sis.'

Catherine felt sad as the train pulled away. She wished that she could see her sister more often. They had always been close, like best friends. And, at the moment, Emma was the only person who believed there was something spooky going on in the house.

CHAPTER 11

*C*atherine sent Adam a text:

What time you setting off back? Xxx

About 5 mins, will be home in about an hour Xxx

Okay. See you soon Xxx

Catherine had one final hour of peace. She made herself a Cadbury's hot chocolate and put some marshmallows on top from her hidden stash. If Bella cottoned on that she had these they wouldn't last very long, so they remained hidden among Catherine's baking equipment. She set it down on the coffee table and popped upstairs to put her phone on charge. She came back downstairs and walked into the living room, stopping dead in her tracks in the doorway.

There he was, just sitting in the armchair. White hair scruffy on his head. Same tatty cardigan with holes in the sleeves. Same pale skin and brown eyes staring into the cold and empty fireplace. Catherine didn't know what to do. She couldn't do anything. She couldn't lift her legs to walk, couldn't open her mouth to speak, barely remembered to breathe. The hairs on the back of her neck and arms were all standing up. She could feel her heart pounding hard in her chest, the room so silent that she could hear every beat. She wished that time would speed up and Adam would walk through the door to help her but he was still a while away yet. What could she do?

'Gone.' He spoke. It was a quiet and delicate voice. Not threatening in any way. He didn't seem to notice Catherine standing in the doorway. 'They've gone.'

She felt less worried after he spoke and relaxed a little, able to ask, 'Wh-who?' She took a deep breath. 'Who has gone?'

'They've gone.'

His eyes remained staring at the fireplace but Catherine noticed how sad he looked. She stepped backwards and into the hall. She needed to get her phone from upstairs. Now he was sitting in the room and speaking, she was sure he wasn't a ghost. How could he be? At least he was in the house so she could phone the police to come and collect him, and find out once and for all where he lived.

'Just stay there, sir. Please just stay where you are, I'll be right back.'

She quickly ran up the stairs to grab her mobile. She didn't even think to go for the house phone in the kitchen. She yanked the mobile so hard she almost pulled the plug out of the socket. Running back onto the landing she tried to unlock it, but her hands were shaking so much that she dropped it and the back came off. Once reassembled, she got to the top of the stairs and looked down to see the front door was wide open. Had he gone out? She ran down and into the living room, but he wasn't there. She looked into the kitchen and the back room and again he was not there. She looked out to the garden and couldn't see him. Where had he gone?

≈

PC Shackleton made notes on his Blackberry with details of Catherine's visitor. The police had been out searching the area but to no avail. Adam was furious that Catherine had left the front door unlocked. Even though it was a harmless old man who had come in, it could have been anyone. Catherine was adamant that she had locked it but clearly she hadn't. Once PC Shackleton finally left and Bella was tucked in bed, Adam and Catherine could talk.

'What happened this morning?'

'When?' Adam asked.

'You know when. You came down this morning and looked like you'd seen a ghost.'

Adam shuffled uncomfortably in his seat.

'It was nothing, I told you, must have been a dream. It felt so real though…'

He told Catherine what had happened. How he'd rolled over after she had left the room and quickly fallen back to sleep but was woken by something. He'd opened his eyes and seen the silhouette of a woman by the window, looking outside. As he'd presumed it was Catherine he'd closed his eyes again only to instantly reopen them when he realised that she would have been downstairs. But the figure had disappeared.

'Eyes play tricks on you all the time when you're tired, so I wasn't sure it was anything. That's what I thought, but there was something different about the air in the room. I can't describe it, but I couldn't stay there. I had to get up. I was still partly convinced that it was you, but when I saw you sitting there and you denied being upstairs I just felt sick. I didn't want to say anything in front of Emma but… for a minute I could have been convinced that it was a ghost stood in the corner of the room.'

Catherine was stunned that he was admitting this. It made it easier to tell him about seeing a silhouette of a girl in the doorway and then hearing the giggling from Bella's room on her way back to bed last night.

'Seriously though,' he began, 'do you really think there is a ghost in the house?'

'Well, I've seen a young girl, you've seen a woman, and we've both seen the disappearing old man. What do you think?'

CHAPTER 12

April 1916

*I*t was a Sunday morning at the start of a new month. The sun was shining and the sky was a perfect ocean of blue. It was unusually warm for a spring morning as Michael made his way to the house. His leg still brought him some pain but he was now able to manage with his wooden limb and stick. In his other hand he carried a small wicker basket which contained a freshly baked apple pie covered over with a small white cloth. He hadn't made it, of course. An elderly neighbour had seen his struggle since returning from the war so regularly brought him food, just like she did after his mother died.

When Michael got to the top of the path to the house he needed to rest for a few minutes. He had been walking too fast. Although the pain was limited, it still took a lot of effort on the cobbled streets and uneven walkways. He struggled to balance, leaning on the wall with his stick in one hand and the basket in the other. He spotted Mary in the garden hanging out sheets to dry. She had seen him but did not return his wave. He was hoping that she would help and take the basket from his hands but she carried on with her duties, ignoring his struggle. He pulled himself back up and walked to the house.

'Michael,' Elizabeth said as she answered the door. She took the basket from him so he could use his newly freed hand to pull himself through the doorway. 'I'm so glad you've come back today. We have so much to do. Are you okay? How's your dad doing?'

Elizabeth had invited Michael to the house for the day to help with a few jobs as Henry had requested in one of his last letters. 'It would be good for him to do some manual work to get used to it,' Henry had written. Elizabeth agreed. Michael would need to go out to work eventually so it was best for him to start now for practice. She had planned a whole day of work but would give him breakfast first; she knew he wouldn't have eaten much at home, if anything.

'I'm well, thank you. My dad is the same really. That basket is for you.' He pulled out a chair and sat himself down at the dining table. 'Mrs Ryder brought us an apple pie but my dad won't want it, so I thought you and the children would like it after your tea tonight.'

'That's very thoughtful of you, Michael, thank you. But you'll be staying for tea too, won't you? I can't have you working here all day and then send you away hungry,' she said with a laugh. 'Will your dad be okay without you all day?'

'Yes, I made him some sandwiches which will see him through, but he'll be asleep most of the day anyway.'

'Well then–' She put her hand on his shoulder which made him blush slightly; he was not used to a woman's touch whatever the situation. '–how about some breakfast?'

～

'I want to butter the toast!' Charlotte shouted at the dining table. 'It's my turn, I want to do it!'

'Toast,' Toby said loudly. He pointed to the toast in the wooden rack. 'Toast.' Charlotte laughed as he called out 'toast' a few more times. Mary scolded her for shouting and handed Toby some toast.

'Charlotte, listen to your sister and don't be rude in front of Michael.' Elizabeth joined them at the table, bringing a bowl of boiled eggs.

'Kull,' Toby said suddenly, pointing at Michael. 'Kull.'

Michael sat uncomfortably. He was not used to children and didn't know what to say back to Toby.

'He's trying to say your name, Michael,' Elizabeth said. 'He must like you!'

'Kull!' he said a little louder.

Elizabeth laughed and motioned at Michael to encourage him to interact with Toby. Michael looked around shyly, not sure what to say to this small child with big blue eyes staring directly at him.

'Err,' he began, 'it's Michael. Michael.'

'Kull!'

'No, no, Michael. My-kull.'

'Kull!'

'My, say my.'

'My!'

'Now kull.'

'Kull!'

'Yes, now say My-kull'

'My. Kull. My-kull. My-kull!' he shouted. 'My-kull!'

'Yes, baby boy!' Elizabeth beamed at her son. 'You did it!' She turned to Michael. 'He has never said more than one syllable before, this is so exciting. I can't wait to write to Henry to tell him. He'll be so proud of his boy. You'll have a friend for life now with Toby.'

'Yay, Toby can speak! He can speak, he can speak,' Charlotte sang loudly.

'And you speak too much!' Mary said to her sister. She put her toast down on her plate. 'I have work to do.' She got up and walked away from the table, glaring at Michael as she left, which went unnoticed by everyone but Michael, as they were too busy fussing around Toby. She didn't like him, this was clear, but he couldn't understand why.

The rest of the family and Michael finished their breakfasts and Elizabeth designated jobs for them all. Mary would look after Toby most of the day keeping him out of trouble; they could pick vegetables from the garden. Charlotte would begin on laundry, overlooked by Elizabeth to make sure she got the hang of it. Michael would be out in the garden: eggs needed to be collected and the chicken coop cleaned, and the hedges had been neglected since Henry left so he would need to trim these down as well as generally tidying up the garden. It would take him most of the day but he was happy to be busy.

It had been a long day for Michael. He was not used to being up and about on his leg for so many hours. He wasn't feeling as much pain from it anymore, as the wound had healed, but his muscles were now tired. He had tidied the garden, trimmed the hedge, helped the children with collecting vegetables and even slaughtered a chicken, which had been prepped for cooking. He finished his day by sitting with Toby and Charlotte watching the sun begin to set.

It was starting to get chilly so he picked up a sleepy Toby and they walked into the house. Michael didn't notice that he'd not used his walking stick. They found Mary setting the table and Elizabeth at the stove, cooking.

'Will you three wash your hands, please?' Elizabeth asked, smiling at Michael. 'Dinner will be ready in a few minutes.'

They did as they were bid and all sat down at the table. Both younger children wanted to sit on either side of Michael.

'Would you like me to do anything?' he asked.

'No, thank you.' She smiled at his new-found popularity. 'I think we're all done. I've made a chicken stew for us to have with some bread and then we can have your apple pie for dessert. I've put it in the oven to warm up.'

Michael thought the smell of the pie heating up was divine. Seeing Elizabeth working in the kitchen and the aromas of all the food cooking reminded him of when his mother was alive. After she'd died he was lucky to get some jam as a treat with his bread. It was not his father's fault. He was out all day getting any work he could find, which was usually on the farms in the summer months and in the mills in winter.

After dinner was finished and most of the apple pie had been eaten Elizabeth sent the children to bed. Michael felt like he could go to sleep for a week. A full day of work and a tummy full of food were a recipe for a good night's rest.

Michael was on the sofa when Elizabeth came in from checking the children. She lightly touched his arm to wake him.

'Michael? It's getting late.'

He opened his eyes to find her standing before him, her face glowing in the light from the candles and fire. Michael noticed how beautiful she looked and almost forgot where he was.

'Sorry,' he said, noticing the clock was showing ten. 'I should go.'

'Will you be okay? It's very dark out now.'

Michael looked out the window. 'The moon's full and the sky is clear; I'll be fine.'

Elizabeth walked with him down the garden path. Even though this was a favour for her husband she was very grateful for Michael's company. She bid him goodnight and watched him walk away, secretly willing him to look back at her before he was out of sight.

My dearest husband,

You will be pleased to know that Michael is making wonderful progress. He no longer struggles as much on his legs. Your idea for him to help at the house has really worked. He has spent a few days here, now, doing various jobs. He has been helping Toby with his speech and Toby is doing so much better. You will be surprised by how much he has come on in such a short space of time. Charlotte loves having Michael in the house. She doesn't tease him as much as I thought she would, and he is getting used to how loud she and Toby can be together. Mary on the other hand still doesn't seem to like him but I don't understand why. I worry that she is unkind to him when I am not around but Michael is too polite to say. Maybe a letter from you would help.

Michael speaks of his father and that he is very ill. I promised that I would visit soon to see if I can be of any help, but he sounds like a stubborn old man. He should probably be in hospital but he refuses to go. I don't know what I will be able to do but I will try my best for Michael's sake. If not, then you will need to pay him a call when you return, whenever that might be.

There is nothing else to report here, really. I seem to be constantly busy at the moment. I have lots of clothes to be mending; Reverend Cuthbert keeps sending them my way. I think he is doing it out of kindness knowing that you are away and that I might need the distraction, but I may have to ask him to limit what he sends. I am falling behind with the housework; there is only so much I can ask the girls to do. It is a good thing I have Michael around to help where he can.

Write to me soon.

Yours,

Liz.

CHAPTER 13

*I*t was mid-April, around noon, and Michael had just arrived at the house. He had not been for a few days as he was caring for his father, but today he would be bringing Elizabeth back with him to see if she could help. He wasn't sure what she would be able to do but since she was a doctor's wife, he hoped she might know a few ways to help his father.

'Good afternoon, Michael,' Elizabeth said as she opened the door. Her long, dark hair was flowing freely, and she was wearing a red floral dress with a white apron. Michael once again noticed how beautiful she was.

'Hello, Elizabeth.' He removed his hat. 'I hope you don't mind doing this today. It's just, his legs are really swollen, the sores look infected, and I don't know what to do.'

'I don't mind, Michael. I don't know what I can do either but, you never know, I might be able to convince him to go to the hospital at least.' She handed him a basket. 'Will you hold this whilst I get my coat?'

'Of course I will.' He took the basket which was covered in a blue flannel cloth. He could smell the freshly baked goods underneath.

'It's just some bread Mary baked. I thought your dad might like some.'

'That's very kind of you, thank you.'

They set off to Michael's house. It wasn't far. He lived in the centre of the village in a small cottage. They spent the whole walk talking about each of their childhoods. Michael wanted to know all about his new friend who had been so kind to him the last few weeks. Growing up it had only been him and his father after his mother had died. He didn't go to school so didn't have any friends. He was not used to people being kind to him. It hadn't been until he joined the army that he spent time in a crowd of people. He'd been beginning to gain some confidence when the incident happened and he lost his leg. Michael had considered ending his life and then he met Henry. Henry was a very kind man and looked after him following the amputation. He felt that he would be letting Henry down if he killed himself so he became determined to recover.

'Henry is very popular in the village, especially with the elderly female patients. They were always giving him cakes and pies to bring home.'

'He is very well liked over there too, at the front. You must miss him a lot.'

'I do, it's been quite lonely, and who knows when he'll be back.'

She looked across to Michael and met his gaze. She noticed how lovely his eyes were, as blue as a summer sky. She felt uncomfortable, somewhat awkward, as though what was happening was inappropriate. She blushed and looked away from his gaze hoping he hadn't noticed her rosy cheeks.

'Is this the house?' She was looking at an old run-down cottage. You could have been forgiven for thinking it was abandoned. The window frames were black with muck and the door plagued with spiders' webs. The windows too filthy with dust to see through properly but clear enough to show the yellowed net curtains. 'I think you might need to do some cleaning here, Michael.'

'I've tried, but he won't let me. He's too stubborn and doesn't like anything to change. It's been like this since my mum died.'

Elizabeth wasn't confident that the inside would be much better. Michael opened the door and they both walked in. She was faced with a smell similar to that of the chicken coop after a few days. It was overpowering but whatever it was it was not from chickens. Michael's father was asleep in an armchair. She guessed that this was where he slept at night too, judging by the state of it and the blanket that he was under. His bare legs were visible through the holes in the blanket, too swollen to fit into trousers. He had cut off the trouser legs himself by the looks of it. Elizabeth could see the sores which covered them and presumed that these were where the smell was coming from. The skin on his legs was splitting and oozing a yellow liquid which stained the armchair and carpet. She had never witnessed a sight quite like it.

'Dad?' Michael passed Elizabeth the basket and walked over to his father to wake him up. 'Dad, we have company. This is the doctor's wife, Elizabeth. She's brought you some food. Dad?' He put his hand on his dad's shoulder.

He was not stirring. Elizabeth sensed that something was not right. She put down the basket and quickly went to check his pulse on his wrist. Nothing.

'I'm so sorry, Michael; I think he's died.' She gently put his hand back into his lap. 'I don't think he's been gone very long. He's still warm.'

'What… what do we do?' He ran a hand through his hair, gripping it tightly and biting his lip to stop it from quivering.

'We need to contact the undertakers.' Elizabeth stepped towards him and placed her hand on his arm. 'They're not far from Henry's surgery. I'll go straight there now and see what they can do. Do you want to stay here?'

Michael was quiet, as quiet as he had been when she first met him. He nodded his head. She felt very upset for Michael and his tragically bad luck at such a young age. She hoped this awful event wouldn't set him back now that he'd made such good progress. She wanted to hug him but wasn't sure it would be a good idea.

'I won't be long.' She walked to the door. 'Will you be okay?'

He nodded. Not taking his eyes off his father.

Elizabeth and Michael arrived back at the house in the early evening, once his father's body had been checked over by a locum doctor and taken away. The doctor did not suspect anything had happened other than his body just giving up from years of infection and disease. Michael seemed to be coping well but he was very quiet. Elizabeth thought he might be best with some peace and quiet, so she told Mary to pack a few things for her and the other children and head round to Aunty Ruth's house for the night but be back after breakfast.

Mary was not keen on leaving her mother alone with Michael. 'I don't like it, Mum,' she said. 'It's not right.'

'Mary, I understand your concern, but poor Michael has been through a lot this year and I would say losing his father is probably the last straw for his sanity. He won't get any peace with Charlotte or Toby around wanting his attention. You can come back in the morning and see that everything is okay but for now I need to make sure that Michael is all right.'

Once the children had gone, she took Michael a cup of tea. He was sitting in the living room in the armchair, his elbow on the arm and his hand covering his face. Elizabeth had lost her own parents at a young age, but she still struggled to find the words to comfort him. He was a grown man after all so she didn't want to seem patronising or motherly, but with what he had already been through she wasn't sure how he would cope.

'Michael?' She entered the room slowly. He didn't stir at her voice. 'Michael?' she said a little louder as she got closer. He pulled his hand from his face and seemed embarrassed at the tears on his cheeks. He quickly wiped them away.

'Here, have this.' She handed him the drink and sat opposite him on the couch. 'And don't worry about being upset. The children will be away for the night, so you don't have to worry about being disturbed.'

Michael nodded, but the tears filled his eyes again. He couldn't hold it back. All the physical and mental pain he had felt after he left the war had been kept hidden away from everyone. Whilst he was in the hospital recovering and learning to adapt after losing a leg there had been no sympathy. Tears were uncalled for. 'Be a man.' 'Man up.' 'Have some balls, man.' 'Men do not cry.' He learned how to hold in his feelings because he had to. There was no one to talk to, but now with the death of his father and the kindness of Elizabeth he couldn't hold any of it back, and he cried for everything that he had been through.

'Oh, Michael.' Elizabeth moved off the couch and knelt in front of him putting her hands on his knees. 'Let it out. Cry all you need to. I'm here for you.' She moved up to sit on the arm of the chair so she could put her arms around him. *He looks as though he's never had a hug in his life*, she thought.

They sat together for twenty minutes until Michael finally calmed down. Elizabeth found that she had also got emotional. She was missing Henry but with the children around she never had time to think about him. Even when she wrote her letters to him, the children were always over her shoulder telling her to pass on their messages. She thought about the danger he was facing daily, and how he would never tell her what was really going on around him. But Michael was proof of what was happening.

'I think we need something stronger than tea, don't you?'

'Definitely.' Michael wiped his eyes on his sleeve.

'We have some sherry in one of the cupboards. We save it for Christmas but I don't think anyone would mind if we had a small glass each.'

She pulled herself off the couch and wiped her face with her apron. In the back of one of the kitchen cupboards she found the bottle, along with two small glasses. She poured some out for her and Michael and took the glasses back into the living room. Michael stood up and accepted the drink she handed to him.

'To your father.' She held her glass up and Michael clinked his against hers.

'To Dad, may you finally be at peace.'

They finished their small drink in one go.

'Michael, why don't you stay here tonight? On the couch? I don't think it's a good idea you being home alone after what happened there today. Wait until the morning when it's light.'

'Oh–' He looked around uncomfortably. '–I don't think that would be a good idea. What would people think? I don't mean to be disrespectful, but I don't want people to think... something is going on.'

Elizabeth knew he had a point. This was a small village, and people in small villages knew everyone else's business. However, this wasn't secret or dangerous. Michael was a young man, Elizabeth a married woman. Her husband had suggested this arrangement to help Michael, as everyone knew. Elizabeth was a kind and respected woman so no one would imagine she would bring shame on herself.

'No one will think anything of it. Don't you worry about that, you can't be alone tonight, you need a friend. I'll get us another drink and then we can talk. Will you top up the fire? I think it's about to go out.'

When Elizabeth returned to the room with their topped-up drinks Michael had just finished with the fire. It was glowing nicely and slowly heating up the room. She walked towards him with the drink.

'Here you go.'

'Thank you.' Michael stood and took the drink from her and their eyes met. The room was dark as they had not lit many candles. Elizabeth smiled up at him, her beautiful face glowing in the firelight. He was unfamiliar with the feeling rising inside him, but there was only one thing he wanted to do.

Michael leant down to Elizabeth and let his lips lightly touch hers. He hesitated, waiting for a reaction, not knowing what she would do. She didn't move so he pushed gently towards her and kissed her. His heart was pounding. Should he back off? Should he run? He felt a hand on his arm and thought she was going to push him away, but she held on to him and she kissed him back. Their tongues met as Michael moved his free hand around her waist, his other still holding the glass of sherry. A sudden smash startled them: Elizabeth had dropped her glass. They both jumped back at the realisation of what they were doing.

'I-I'm sorry...' Michael stuttered. 'I'm sorry, I shouldn't have done that.' He moved back almost stepping into the fire. Elizabeth had her hand over her mouth and was shaking.

'That shouldn't have happened. That should not have happened.' She shook her head and then covered her face with both her hands. 'No, no, that was bad.' She turned and ran into the kitchen. Michael followed her.

'Elizabeth, I'm sorry.' He caught up to her and she still had her hands covering her face. 'Please, look at me.' He pulled her arms down from her face and she looked up at him. 'I'm sorry. Please forgive me.'

'It's not your fault.' She looked into his eyes and she knew it was going to happen again. She couldn't help herself. The feeling inside her was too strong to control, and she could tell that he felt the same way. She let him kiss her once more. She didn't think of the consequences. She didn't think of Henry or her children. Not when Michael was holding her tightly or even when they made their way upstairs.

CHAPTER 14

April 2016

It was a rare Sunday for the young family. The sun was shining and it promised to be a warm spring day. On top of that, Adam was off work for a few days and Catherine could spare the day from work too. The three of them were able to spend the whole day out together for the first time since moving in. They planned on going out to the village for the morning and then find somewhere to have lunch. Every Sunday there was a market which attracted a lot of people, so they decided to head there first.

Since Emma's brief visit there had been no further unexplainable activity in the house. The old man had not returned, the young giggling girl had stopped making noises and the woman had not reappeared in their bedroom. Catherine had resigned herself to the fact that her eyes and imagination must have been playing tricks on her and everything in her life was actually ticking over quite nicely. In fact, it could not be more perfect.

Adam and Catherine held hands as they walked together, Bella skipping in front of them singing happily to herself. They strolled down their garden path and onto the lane which led them down to the main road. Traffic was already starting to build as people made their way to the market.

'Janey! It's Janey!' Bella shouted, pointing at her friend who was up ahead holding her mother's hand.

'Bella!' Janey shouted back. The girls ran to each other and began talking excitedly, giving their parents time to catch up.

'Gillian,' Catherine said, smiling. 'It's nice to see you again.'

'Hello, Catherine.' Gillian returned her smile and her eyes then moved to Adam.

'This is my husband Adam. Adam, this is Janey's mum Gillian.'

'Oh, this is the fireman?' She looked him up and down and held out her hand to shake his. 'It's very nice to meet you, Adam.'

'It's nice to meet you too.' He held out his hand in return. She grabbed it, giving the impression she didn't want to let go anytime soon. 'I've heard a lot about Janey, it's nice to finally meet her too,' he said, struggling to pull away from Gillian's grip. Once she realised what she was doing she let him go.

'And where are you guys heading today?' she asked.

'We're just having a wander around,' Catherine said. 'It's the first chance we've had really as a family, and it's a nice day so we didn't want to waste the opportunity.' Catherine managed to regain control of her husband's hand, gripping tightly back on to it.

'Mummy, Janey's going to the swings. Can we go too? Please?'

'There are swings?' Catherine directed this question at Gillian, knowing she would have the answer.

'Yes, it's a secure play area outside a tea room. It's only small but it's good as there's nowhere for the children to go, so you know they're safe while you relax. Why don't you come along? Janey is always talking about Bella. It would be nice for them to see each other outside of school while we're all here together.

Her dad is working today so we decided on a little stroll to keep ourselves entertained.'

Adam shot Catherine a look suggesting he would rather be anywhere else than here with this woman who couldn't take her hungry eyes off him, but glancing at his daughter changed his mind. He thought about how lonely she must have been since moving here and leaving all her friends behind. She must get so bored, especially if she felt the need to create an imaginary friend named Charlotte. An hour wouldn't hurt, surely.

'I think we can manage a coffee,' he said.

'Great,' Gillian said. 'Follow me then.'

Gillian led them through the village and down a small lane. Catherine could see signs pointing to 'Dory's Corner', which was the family-run tea room and play area. You couldn't see the play area, but you could certainly hear it. Catherine noticed the walls around the back of the café; they were six feet high. The sound of children's laughter was coming from inside them. It seemed a bit prison-like but once inside she saw that the walls had been painted like a beach. The bottom was yellow for the sand, the middle dark blue with big waves for the sea and the top a lighter blue for the sky, with clouds and birds. The beach theme continued in the play area. The bars across the top of the swings had various colourful plastic fish hanging down, and there were fish stickers down the slide and actual beach balls in the ball pool and sandpit. It didn't look like much to Catherine, but Bella was amazed. She ran with Janey to the slide, forgetting that her parents were there.

'She'll be fine,' Gillian said, seeing Catherine's look of concern. 'She can't get out anywhere without coming back through the café and we can sit just there in the window.'

They walked back inside together. Adam suggested that he go and get the drinks and then they could sit straight down.

'So, how's it going in the house? Have you settled in?'

'Yes we have, thank you. It's taken some getting used to

having so much space, but we're doing fine. Our new sofa arrived the other day so our living room doesn't look as empty now.'

'Oh, what kind of sofa did you get?'

'It's one of those corner sofas with a recliner on one of the ends. It's so comfortable. Adam fell asleep on it as soon as he got home from work. And we got a single armchair to match too, which Bella has claimed as her throne.'

'It sounds lovely.'

Catherine glanced out the window to check on her daughter, but she was fine. She and Janey were now next to each other on the swings laughing and having fun. Adam soon returned with a tray carrying three hot chocolates and two small cartons of juice for the girls.

'Here we go, ladies, enjoy.'

'Why, thank you.' Gillian took a sip. 'You know, Catherine, when you told me before where you were living I was a bit shocked. That house has always been something of a legend around here with the locals. I could tell you were from out of town as you didn't seem to know anything about it.'

'What do you mean?' Catherine asked. 'What kind of legend?'

'Well, more rumour really, stories from over the years.' Gillian took another sip of her drink, keeping them both in suspense. 'Supposedly, about a hundred years ago, the family living there disappeared whilst the husband was fighting in the First World War. He came back and was traumatised. Went mad looking for them. Apparently the wife ran off with some young farmhand she'd hired to help out, but the husband never found her. They didn't have the internet back then, did they, or he probably would have found her in no time. But she took his kids! So horrible. I'm surprised you haven't heard about it yet, with you being here a few months now.'

'No.' Catherine and Adam looked at each other. 'We've barely been out to speak to anyone. That's so sad.'

'Mmm,' she agreed. 'The kids were only young. I can't

remember their names. Mary, Toby and... I can never remember the other one. But, yeah, that poor man. He died some time ago, obviously, a lonely old man.'

'So, what's the rumour?' Adam asked.

'What do you mean?'

'You said there was a rumour. What is it?'

'Oh, just silly things. People say the old man still haunts the house looking for his family. Just wanders around knocking on doors muttering to himself.' She noticed Catherine and Adam share another look. 'What? What is it? Have you seen him?' she asked eagerly.

'Nothing,' Adam responded. 'We don't believe in any of that. We just don't want Bella to overhear and get scared.'

'Oh, yes,' Gillian agreed, 'sorry! We'll change the subject. So, Catherine, what do you do with your days whilst Adam is out saving lives?'

After a longer than necessary drink and chat with Gillian, the family finally made it to the market to do some browsing around the stalls. They didn't buy anything but it felt nice to be out of Gillian's company. It was good for Catherine to have another person in the area she could talk to, but Adam had found her a little bit irritating. Someone who was always on the lookout for gossip. Once they had browsed around the stalls and then filled up on a pub lunch, they carried a very sleepy Bella home where she had a nap on her throne.

'What Gillian said,' Catherine started, as she stood in the kitchen with Adam, 'you don't suppose... the man, it's a bit weird isn't it? Of all the things to mention.'

'It's a load of rubbish, that's what it is. She was just stirring. Bella has obviously told Janey about our visitor and she's told her mother who saw an opportunity to freak us out. I doubt very much that we're living in a house of scandal. And if this house-wife did run off with a young man to never return, then that's their business. Nothing we can do about it now, is there? I'll just have to make sure I don't hire any young farmers to help out around here and steal you away from me.' He kissed his wife on the cheek and made his way into the living room. Catherine was about to join him when the phone rang.

'Hello?'

'Hello, can I speak to Catherine, please?' said a female voice.

'Yes, speaking.'

'Hello, I'm just enquiring about a cake. My friend Gillian phoned me to tell me you live locally and that you run a business from home. She said she was talking to you today and that you would be able to help me. I had someone lined up, but they've just let me down and I need something for next weekend. I've found your website and your cakes look amazing, exactly what I'm after.'

~

Catherine made her way to the living room with a fresh coffee for Adam.

'Who was that on the phone?' Adam asked, taking his coffee. He could smell the caramel which Catherine had put in to make it sweet.

'A lady who lives about a mile away from here, Bridie some-thing or other. She heard about me from Gillian today and she needs a cake for next weekend. She's coming over tomorrow.'

'Oh, that's good. Bit short notice isn't it, though? Do you have much on this week?'

'Kind of, but depends what she wants really. If you're off work, though, you can sort out Bella with school and I can crack on.'

CHAPTER 15

*B*ridie was a bubbly lady who Catherine liked straight
away. She was in her late fifties and a retired teacher
from Bella's school. She came through the door and Catherine
noticed her potted arm.

'I usually make all the cakes for my grandchildren's birthdays
but as you can see–' She held out her potted arm. '–I'm having a
spot of bother. I did it months ago for the first time while
cleaning out our caravan. We own a static over in Settle you see,
dear.' Catherine ushered her into the kitchen and to the table.
'Anyway, I slipped in some mud and landed on my arm and it
broke, of course. Then a few weeks ago as it was healing, I took
the dog for a walk who decided to pull me along and I fell over
the root of a tree. Snap, again. Unbelievable.'

'Oh dear, you're not having much luck with that arm. Do you
want to take a seat and I'll bring you a drink?'

'Could I just have some water? I've walked around here from
home and I feel like I'm on fire.' She pulled off her coat and scarf
and set it on the back of the chair. Catherine brought them both a
glass of water and opened her portfolio and notebook.

'So, what is it you're wanting exactly?' She clicked her pen, ready to jot down some ideas. 'It's a bit short notice, but I'm sure I can whip something together for you. Was it something for your grandchild?'

'Oh, yes. Daniel will be ten this weekend and his mum is having a small party at their house for him. I love baking; I've done it most of my life. Everyone always assumes that I'll make the cakes now, but if I go back to the hospital with this arm they'll start charging me.' She laughed. It was a great, infectious chuckle. 'So, I have no choice but to step back and let someone else do it, which will be so hard. But when Gillian called me yesterday to tell me about you, it was like fate. I was straight on your website and have to say I loved the one you did where each tier was a different colour like a rainbow. He would love that.'

'Yes, I remember that.' Catherine flicked through her folder and found the designs. 'Here it is. I actually had a thought on this, after I did it, to remove some of the centre and fill it with Smarties. Then when it's cut into, the Smarties all fall out. It was too late last time, so I said to myself next time that's what I'd do.'

'Ooh, even better! All the cakes I've made all seem so boring and unoriginal compared to some of yours.' She studied the designs and smiled. 'I love this idea though. Would there be icing around it?'

'It can be icing if you like or buttercream or chocolate. Anything at all.'

'Well, I'll tell you what, my dear–' She put down the drawings and put her hand on Catherine's. '–you do me a cake that I can come and collect Friday night and I'll let you choose how it's done. As long as it'll be enough for, say, twenty people then you're definitely hired. How can I not hire you?'

'That's great, thank you. I'll start working on it today, but I can have it ready for Friday, no problem.'

'Perfect.' Bridie took a drink of her water. 'Well, I'll leave you to it. Call me if you need to, won't you?'

'Course, thank you. Oh, actually I do have a question, a non-cake-related question.'

'Yes, my dear?'

'It's about the house. This house. Gillian seemed to think there was some sort of history with the house and some kind of haunting. I just wondered if you knew anything about it?'

'Oh, don't let Gillian scare you with these stories. All old houses have a history. That's the beauty of them. The only difference between this house and the one down the road is that the history of this house was made public and so everyone knows about it. The poor man, though.'

'Gillian mentioned about an old man, and it made me curious.' Catherine knew Adam wouldn't approve of her asking. He would say she was trying to scare herself, but she had to know more about it. 'What happened?'

'Well, I remember seeing him when I was a child just before he died. Supposedly he was a well-respected doctor when he was younger and a very handsome man. When she snapped him up it made all the young women jealous. Elizabeth, that was the wife, it was her family house. Abberton, who built it, was her grandfather. Anyway, you wouldn't have thought he was handsome before he died. His clothes were always tatty, his white hair always messy and he was smelly too. Didn't know how to look after himself in the end. Refused any help. If anyone tried to reach out to him he sent them away to look for his family instead. He never wanted to believe that they left him. He thought something more sinister had happened.'

'Like what?'

'Anything that would have been different from his wife taking their children and running away with a younger man. Who would want to accept that? Those poor kids, they never went back to see him. They would have been old enough to remember him. Well, Toby might have been too young but Mary and Charlotte had no excuse.'

'Did you say Charlotte?' Something about that name was familiar to Catherine but she couldn't remember what.

'Yes, that was the older... no, middle child. Yes she was definitely the middle child. Mary the eldest and Toby was still a baby, I think. And now you know the story. So you can pass it on to the next generation and so on, like the rest of us.' She laughed, getting to her feet to put on her coat and scarf. 'Thank you so much again, and I will pop back on Friday with my husband. It'll probably be around seven o'clock, is that okay?'

'That's great, yes. It will be ready and boxed for you then.'

They walked to the door together, Catherine still thinking about the name, even after Bridie had left.

Adam returned not long after with Bella who ran straight into the living room and onto her throne.

'Not so fast, madam. Go wash your hands first, they're filthy.'

'But, Dad! I'm on my throne. I'm the Queen. You can't tell me what to do.' She giggled.

'Oh, yeah? Well, I heard that queens aren't ticklish. So, if I tickle you and you don't squirm around and laugh then you can stay there.' He headed towards her, hands poised like claws, Bella still giggling. 'Ready? One... two...' He had her, tickling her under her arms where he knew it would drive her mad.

'No, Daddy, no!' She laughed and squirmed and tried to fight back but it was a losing battle.

'Hmm, I don't think you are a queen really. Do you, Mummy?'

'Definitely not!' Catherine said, welcoming the distraction from her thoughts about the name 'Charlotte'.

Bella put up a good fight but she had to give in. Adam kissed her on the head and left her to run upstairs to the bathroom to wash the muck off her hands.

'So how did it go with Birdy? Must have been a quick meeting.' He sat down next to his wife and put his arm around her.

'It's Bridie, not Birdy, you wally. It was a very quick meeting but it's all arranged. Won't take me long to do. I'll get it started tomorrow for her. She's really nice, used to be a teacher. Sounds a bit clumsy though. She's broken her arm in the same place twice already this year.'

'Bloody hell, that's an achievement.'

'Yeah, said she wants the rainbow cake for her grandson. Like the one I did for your work friend's son last year.'

Adam could tell there was something on her mind. She was usually a bit more excited when she got a new client. He thought she would have been extra happy at having someone from the village requesting one of her cakes, as it meant word would spread and bring in more business.

'What's the matter? Why aren't you happy?'

'I am, it's just... who's Charlotte?'

'Charlotte?' he said, puzzled by the random question. 'I've no idea.'

'Bridie mentioned a Charlotte and I can't remember why or where I heard that name recently. Is it someone Bella goes to school with?'

'Bella said her imaginary friend was Charlotte. You know, when your sister was here and we were stood outside. Why? What's this got to do with anything?' Catherine's face had gone slightly pale. 'What is it? What's up?'

She told Adam what Bridie had said about the family, the names of the children and the old man.

'Catherine, this is getting ridiculous. You're going to drive yourself mad with this.' He stood up. 'So we've had the ghost of the doctor in the house and Bella is upstairs playing with the ghost of his daughter? Do you realise how daft this sounds?'

'It's a bit of a coincidence, don't you think?'

'That's exactly what it is,' he said loudly, 'a coincidence. Nothing more.'

'My hands are clean now.' Bella was standing in the doorway. She had stopped with her giggles and was looking at her dad, eyes bright and confused as to why he seemed angry.

'Good girl,' he lowered his tone and quickly changed it back to playful, 'now why don't we go find something for tea? And maybe after, you can have ice cream, yes?'

'Okay, Daddy!' She beamed and ran into the kitchen.

'I'll be right there.' He looked down at his wife on the couch. They rarely argued so he felt incredibly guilty at how he'd reacted. 'I'm sorry, really. I didn't mean to shout.' He knelt down in front of Catherine and held her hands. 'I just don't like the idea of you alone in the house all day thinking these thoughts and scaring yourself. The last thing you want is me away on a night shift and believing there's a ghost in the house. It's all history and rumours which we can't change. Promise me you'll let it go.'

'I promise. It's just a little weird with what happened the night Emma was here and the name Charlotte popping up like that. I'll forget it now.'

'Nothing else has happened. We are just settling into a new house and getting used to all its creaks and bumps. It's nothing.'

'Dad!' Bella shouted from the kitchen. 'I'm hungry!'

'Coming, princess.' He kissed his wife's hands and ran to the kitchen to join his daughter.

CHAPTER 16

*F*riday came around all too quickly for Catherine. She had so much to do that she was grateful to have Adam at home at the start of the week. He had gone back to work on Wednesday but having him around had given her the chance to catch up on her orders. She not only had Bridie's but two others which needed completing too.

'You'll make yourself ill,' Adam had said to her on Tuesday. 'Let me help you.'

'You're helping enough by sorting out Bella for me. Seriously, I'm fine. What do you want for tea tonight?'

'I'll sort out tea. Don't worry about that,' he insisted.

'No, this is supposed to be your time off work to relax, not to be my house husband.'

'Just because you're at home doesn't mean you're a housewife.' He kissed her on the cheek. 'You're working, I'm not. Fish and chips for tea. No arguments. I'll take Bella with me to get them and then I'm washing up, okay?'

At times, she couldn't believe how lucky she was to have Adam as her husband. There wasn't a selfish bone in his body. She would listen to her friends moan about their own husbands and boyfriends being lazy with the housework and acting like children, but she never had anything to complain about. She knew her friends were envious of her.

Adam was right when he said that she would end up making herself ill. On Friday morning, whilst walking home from taking Bella to school, she suddenly felt light-headed and needed to steady herself on the garden wall. She had half an hour before Chloe came to collect the fifty muffins she had ordered for a baby shower. Bridie's cake was also finished and ready for collection, so once the muffins were gone she could relax for a few hours and catch up on some sleep.

~

'Oh you are pale today, Cat. Are you not well?' Chloe Stevens was a friend of Catherine's from college. She lived just on the outskirts of Keighley and always used her services when cake was needed. 'I think you need to go to bed. Where's Adam?'

'He's in bed. He's on nights and starts at lunchtime today so I don't want to wake him, he'll only worry. I've so much on this week I've just let it get on top of me.'

'You should have said, hun. I could have helped with these.' She pointed at the muffins. 'I could have decorated them; they don't need to be perfect.'

'No, it's fine, seriously. I'm used to the workload. I must just have a virus coming on or something making me tired and dizzy.'

'Well make sure you put your feet up this weekend. Why don't I take Bella tomorrow night? She can sleep with Becky in her room. They had fun last time.'

'That's really kind of you, thank you. If I didn't have my parents coming for dinner on Sunday I would let you take her.'

'Oh, they're coming?' Chloe knew Catherine's parents very well. More so her mother. 'No wonder you're feeling ill.'

'Tell me about it.'

'Okay.' She picked up the box of muffins. 'Take care of yourself, put your feet up, and call me if you need me.'

'I will. It's been good to see you. Stay for a coffee next time.'

They hugged and promised to make more time for each other, as they always did. Truth be told, it had been a few years since they had seen each other properly for a catch-up. A couple of times a year Chloe would order a cake for an occasion but neither of them had time to hang out. Last year Catherine and Adam had needed someone to watch Bella for the night while they were away for a wedding, so Chloe volunteered since Adam's parents weren't available.

Catherine's parents lived in Alnwick, so it wasn't convenient for them. Bella didn't know them well, really, as they never made much time to visit. They were both retired and spent most of their free time abroad, which to Catherine felt like twelve months of the year. She wasn't close to her parents at all. She and her mother had a very icy relationship, something she vowed would never happen between her and Bella. It had reached its peak when Catherine had said she would not be going to university. They'd wanted her to study in Scotland, like they did, and qualify as a doctor, but Catherine never had that kind of ambition. She was more artistic and creative, not academic. She always felt that they resented her choices and that she'd settled down with a fireman. They never truly warmed to Adam and had refused to visit when they lived in the apartment. Now they owned a house, however, her parents had agreed to come.

'That is absolutely splendid, Catherine.' Bridie beamed as she was presented with her grandson's birthday cake. Catherine had opted for a simple white icing cake. There were two round tiers. She wanted to give the illusion that it was a plain, boring cake before the magic on the inside was revealed.

'There are five different coloured layers in the bottom tier and three more on top. And in the centre of the bottom tier, I've made space for Smarties so when he cuts into it they will all fall out.'

'He will love it, won't he, John?' Bridie said to her husband who was standing beside her. 'His mum will love it too. Thank you ever so much.'

'It's no problem at all.' Catherine loved to see her work appreciated. Especially by someone like Bridie who knew about baking.

'How much is it, my dear?'

'Call it £60 for that one.'

'Is that all? I saw other companies offering something half as good for twice as much.'

'Well, just promise me you'll spread the word that I'm here and help me get some more clients. Once your arm is healed you'll be back in business and won't need me again.'

'I don't know about that now I've seen what you can do. I'll be keeping you on standby myself or coming around for some ideas.'

'You're welcome anytime. Just give me a call, if you like?'

'That is kind of you, thank you. John? Would you take this out to the car and I can pay Catherine?'

'Right-o.' He lifted the boxed cake and made his way out through the door. Bridie gave Catherine the money.

'Are you okay, my dear? You're awfully pale today,' she observed. 'Looks like you need to put your feet up.'

'I am a bit tired and could be tempted to go to bed very soon. I've got a busy weekend, so I need my strength.'

'Well, make sure you do just that, I insist.' They walked to the door and Catherine waved as they drove away.

She made her way to join Bella in the living room. Bella had been very well behaved. Usually, when there were visitors, Bella loved to introduce herself or make herself known in some way, but today she had been very quiet.

'Are you okay, princess? What are you watching?' Catherine sat on the arm of Bella's throne.

'It's *Finding Nemo*,' Bella said.

'Again? You've watched it twice already this week. If you start swimming around the house I'll know why.'

Bella laughed. 'It's funny. I love Dory. Oh!' She jumped up excitedly. 'Can we go back to Dory's Corner tomorrow? Please, please, please?'

'I'm sorry, princess, I've got too much to do with Grandma and Granddad coming to visit on Sunday, and with your dad working I need to give the house a good clean.' Catherine's mother was very good at spotting even the tiniest speck of dust so she had to be extremely thorough with her cleaning. 'We'll go another time, okay?'

'Okay.' Bella slumped back into her chair to watch the rest of her film.

'Come here.' Catherine got up and sat in the armchair pulling Bella to sit on her lap. 'Come on, let's watch this together, eh? Shall we start it from the beginning?'

It was a little after one in the morning when Adam pulled up to the house. It had been an easy shift, stress free, which was odd for a Friday night in Bradford, but he wasn't going to complain. He only had one more shift on Saturday and then he was free for a couple of days. He wasn't looking forward to his Sunday off work though; it wouldn't be very relaxing. He hadn't seen his in-laws for some time but they never treated him with any respect. To them, Catherine had married beneath herself. He and Catherine had met each other at college when Adam was in his final year. He never went to university either. He knew what career he wanted. If the role of Batman wasn't available then he would be a fireman. That's what he'd told Catherine's father on their first meeting. Their relationship had dwindled from then on.

As he got out of the car he spotted that the downstairs lights were on. This didn't bother him as it gave the impression to burglars that there was someone at home. However, he could hear his grandfather's voice bellowing in his ear, 'It's like Blackpool Illuminations in here!' It was odd for Catherine to leave all the lights on, though. She usually left the odd lamp on but never much else.

He crept in quietly through the door, closing it gently behind him. He took off his boots and went to the kitchen to put the kettle on. He never went straight up to bed after a shift, as he was never tired enough and always liked to have a cup of tea and watch TV first to try to wind down.

He picked up his drink and the sandwich that Catherine had left for him in the fridge. When he walked into the living room he didn't notice them at first. But his heart felt like it skipped a beat as he noticed Catherine and Bella cuddled up together on the armchair, fast asleep. He was jealous that he wasn't involved. Had they been on the sofa he'd have been very tempted to join them.

He very carefully picked up Bella and carried her to bed. She didn't stir. When he got back to the living room Catherine had woken up.

'Hi, baby,' Adam said softly. 'Are you okay? I've just carried Bella up to bed.'

'I thought you might have. I don't know what happened. I must have needed that sleep.'

'Take yourself up to bed, or do you need me to carry you too?'

'Ha-ha, I think I can manage.' She kissed her husband goodnight and made her way upstairs.

CHAPTER 17

The dreaded day had arrived. It was Sunday which meant Catherine's parents were on their way. They were due to arrive from Alnwick at two o'clock. Adam was secretly hoping that they would get caught up in all the traffic caused by the Sunday market and be late. The less time they were around the better. Adam knew that this was the reason why Catherine had been so ill during the week. She had let herself get stressed out that her mother would find a fault in their home. Her mother was always criticising them in some way, nothing was ever good enough. Adam would do his best to not let that happen this time. He was up early despite working the night before to ensure he could help his wife with all the last-minute preparations. They were going to have a Sunday roast followed by pudding and then, Adam hoped, her parents would leave not long after. That was the plan.

'That's their car. They're early. Shit!' Catherine was still in the middle of peeling potatoes as they pulled up outside. 'Look at the mess!' Potato skins had made their way onto the floor.

'Go take Bella and greet them. I'll sort this out and finish it off. Go on.' He took the potato peeler from Catherine and gave her a towel to dry her hands.

'Okay, okay, thank you. Bella,' she called to the living room, 'come on, princess, let's go and say hello.'

Catherine opened the door and she and Bella made their way down the path to the car. The path had never felt like such a long walk before. It had rained all night and there were puddles everywhere.

'Hi, Mum,' she said as she reached her mother who was climbing out of their new Mercedes. 'How was the drive over?'

'Hello, darling.' She put her face to one side so Catherine could kiss her on the cheek. Such a formal routine of theirs. Whenever Catherine saw Adam's mother she was always met with a huge, tight hug, but never from her own. It was always a kiss on the cheek and no embracing or affection.

'Hello, Catherine.' Her father never failed to hug his daughter whenever he saw her. 'What is with all that traffic? It's absolutely manic.'

'There's a market every Sunday. I should have told you. It does get really busy at times.' She remembered Bella by her side. 'Say hello, Bella.'

'Hi, Grandma. Hi, Granddad.'

'Hello, poppet,' Catherine's father said to her. 'Come here now.' He picked her up for a cuddle and then carried her towards the house. 'Is this where you live? Oh it's very pretty, isn't it? Nice and big.' This left Catherine and her mother to walk together.

'What do you think of the house, Mum?'

'I haven't seen inside yet,' she said, bluntly. 'I'll tell you when I've looked properly. Those shutters have to go, though. Hideous.'

Catherine loved the blue shutters on the windows and had no intention of removing them. In fact, in the summer, she would be sprucing them up with some fresh paint.

'Colin.' Adam had come to the door to greet his in-laws. 'It's good to see you.' They shook hands.

'Hello, Adam. Thank you for having us. We're thrilled to be here, aren't we, Linda?' he said, gesturing to his wife as they all entered the kitchen. She was looking around as though not paying attention to the conversation.

'Is that the dining room through there?' She pointed to the room at the back of the kitchen.

'No, Mum, that's where I do all my work. You know, cake decorating and such. The dining table is in here, see?'

'Didn't you tell me there was a conservatory? Why can't you have the table in there? Wouldn't it be so much nicer than eating in here?' She looked around the kitchen and at the units on the wall. 'I'll bet it's filthy on top of there. No one ever thinks to clean up there. Why would I want to eat in here when there could be something going mouldy up there?'

'The conservatory was built before the central heating was installed,' Adam interjected, seeing Catherine was beginning to lose patience. 'So it's too cold to sit comfortably and eat in there. We might do one day if we can get some radiators put in.'

'It just seems a waste, that's all. All this downstairs space and no separate dining room.'

'I think my room at the back was originally a dining room but we didn't really need one and it comes in really handy for me to have my own space. I've so many orders to do I'm hardly out of there lately.'

Catherine tried to laugh to lighten the mood, but her mother showed no signs of any humour on her stone-cold face.

'Well, Bella.' Colin was still holding Bella in his arms. 'Why don't you give us a tour of the house and your mummy and daddy can finish up in here, okay?'

Dinner was a success, surprisingly, Catherine thought. That is the food was a success, not so much the company. Conversation was flowing between Adam and Colin who were discussing property value and investments. Bella was trying her hardest to talk to her grandma but even she could tell it was a lost cause.

'The food was delicious, Catherine. Well done,' Colin said, rubbing his belly and resisting the urge to undo his belt. 'I've barely got room for dessert.'

'Thank you, Dad, that's really nice to hear.'

'The potatoes hadn't been boiled for long enough before you put them into roast,' her mother piped up. 'I had one or two that were a tad too crunchy. You must have rushed them.'

Adam reached out to hold his wife's hand, which was on the table scrunching up a napkin with frustration. 'Why don't Bella and I tidy away the plates,' he quickly said, 'and you can get the pudding out of the oven, Cat?'

Bella did as she was bid without saying a word. Adam spied Colin giving his wife a disapproving look. He often had to, but in all the years that Adam had known them it had never made a difference to how she treated her daughter.

'What's for dessert, Catherine?' she asked, as she rearranged the napkin on her lap.

'I've made an apple pie. It's Adam's mum's recipe. I made the custard too, from scratch.'

'Well, isn't that lovely?' she gave a patronising smile. Catherine knew that her mother was quick to get jealous when it came to Adam's mum. It all started at their wedding. Adam's mum had been so involved in the wedding preparations compared with Linda. She went to dress fittings, helped find a venue and contributed towards the overall cost. Then on the day of the wedding, as Catherine walked down the aisle, she cried. Linda hadn't cried, she never did, but seeing another woman get so emotionally involved in her daughter's life had probably been hard for her, though she never let anyone know that was how she felt.

Once the pudding was finished they made their way to the

living room to relax with some coffees before Colin and Linda drove back home.

'Your home is wonderful, darling. Very charming,' Colin said. 'I just can't believe the price you got it for. It must have been on the market for a while for them to let it go at your first offer.'

'I think it was only on the market for a few months, but it has been sitting empty for a while. I'm not too sure really.'

'I think I'll just use the bathroom before we leave.' He got up off the sofa. 'I won't be a moment and then we can set off, Linda.' He made his way upstairs.

'Do you think you'll install a downstairs toilet?' Linda asked after a minute of awkward silence.

'Erm–' Catherine and Adam looked at each other. '–we haven't really discussed it but we've only been here a couple of months. We've got a lot we want to do really,' Adam said.

'Oh, okay.' And back to silence.

After a few minutes, Colin came back downstairs.

'I'm not sure what Bella is doing in her room but whatever it is she's having a really good time, giggling away at something. Didn't even reply when I called her name. She is such a lovely little girl.'

'I'm here, Granddad,' Bella said. She had been sitting with a book behind the couch, but was now watching him, confused.

'Oh! So you are! That is really funny. I could have sworn you were up there in your room. Your door was slightly ajar and I distinctly heard laughing.' He looked around the room in confusion, as if hoping to discover that they were winding him up, but they were all looking back at him equally bewildered.

'She's been down here the whole time, Dad.'

'It must have been a toy or a game she's forgotten to switch off,' Adam said.

'I don't think she has any games that laugh,' Catherine said.

'Well, she must have. There's nothing else it could have been. Either that or Colin has finally lost the plot.'

'Ho-ho, young man, very cheeky of you.' Colin laughed. 'I must have been imagining it. Very peculiar.' He rubbed his chin, frowning. 'Okay, my lovely, dearest wife, shall we get off then?'

~

'Are you okay?' Adam asked Catherine as they lay in bed together that night.

'I'm fine, that wasn't as painful as I thought it would be. I'm glad it was only a short visit.' She turned to face Adam. He lifted his arm up so she could snuggle up to him.

'If we're lucky that'll do for visits until Christmas at least. Maybe we should talk them into getting Skype, then they wouldn't need to come over at all.' He snickered. Catherine didn't respond. He hoped she wasn't offended. She usually agreed with him. 'Cat?'

'Sorry, I'm miles away. Just thinking about what my dad said.'

'About the house price being so low?' he asked, not sure what else she could be referring to.

'No, about the laughing in Bella's room. That's what happened when Emma was here.' Adam pulled his arm from under Catherine's body and sat up to look at her.

'Catherine, there's nothing peculiar about that. It was either a toy or his old age playing tricks on him.'

'Old age? He's only sixty!'

'That was a joke, will you lighten up? Just relax. Today is over and done with.' He pulled her back into his side and kissed her head. 'You can chill now and carry on as normal. No more stressing, okay?'

'Okay.' She put her arm around him and they slowly drifted off to sleep together.

She was so exhausted from her busy and stressful week that she fell straight into a dream. She and Bella were in the park and Bella was laughing, but Bella's laugh was loud. It was so loud that it could be heard over the walls of Dory's Corner and she could see people inside the tea room complaining at the noise that Bella was making. She tried to quieten Bella down but it wouldn't work. Suddenly, Catherine was jolted awake.

'What was that?' She heard Adam say.

'I don't know.' She checked her phone for the time. It was after midnight. She had only been asleep for an hour. She looked at Adam who had also been asleep. Had they both heard the same thing? 'I was dreaming about Bella. She was laughing so loudly, I thought that was what woke me up.'

'Well, I don't think I was dreaming, but I could swear I heard a laugh. It was loud; it sounded like it was right outside the door.' He turned to his bedside table to switch on his lamp. They sat in silence staring at the closed door, barely even breathing, but they didn't hear a sound. 'How strange. Must be your father giving us both nightmares.'

'I might go make sure Bella's okay.' Catherine didn't fancy walking across the landing on her own in the dark, but she had to check on her daughter. 'I won't be a minute.'

'Do you want me to come?'

Catherine didn't want to seem as if she was scared of the dark, but having Adam close by would be a comfort. 'Just come with me to turn the light on. It's so dark out there.'

They both got out of bed and walked to the bedroom door. Catherine opened it slowly so it wouldn't make too much noise. The door tended to creak when opened too quickly and she didn't want to wake up Bella. Adam reached out to switch on the landing light and Catherine made her way across to Bella's room. She twisted the handle and opened the door. The night light which glowed in the corner of the room clearly showed Bella was sitting up in bed, awake.

'Mummy?' she said, in a croaky voice as though she had been crying.

'Bella, princess, what's the matter?' Catherine went over to sit on the bed and Bella reached out to cuddle her. 'Why are you awake?'

'I was asleep but Charlotte kept waking me up. Told me to go outside. She wouldn't listen. I cried and she kept laughing at me and said she would go on her own.' Bella was crying again and whatever she said next was inaudible. Hearing the crying Adam came into the room.

'What's happened?' he asked, and sat down next to Bella.

'I think she's been having funny dreams too, like us. Bella, me and Daddy have had some weird dreams too. They woke us up.'

'I wasn't dreaming. Charlotte woke me up. She took Barney off me when I said I wouldn't go with her.'

Catherine looked around the room. Barney was always in bed with Bella but she couldn't see him anywhere. Bella was so upset; it was heart breaking. She hugged her tightly and then thought about the name.

'Did you say Charlotte?'

'Cat…' Adam was shaking his head at her. 'Not now.'

'Yes, Charlotte. I told you before she lives here.' Bella wiped her face on her hand. 'She's always in my room. I knew you wouldn't believe me.'

'Always in your room?' Adam asked, looking around. He wouldn't admit it but this was starting to spook him. Bella never lied. She might be tired and confused but she would never lie to them.

'Yeah. I don't always see her. She just does stuff. Moves stuff. She thinks it's funny. It is funny. But I told her… I said, I can't go outside at night. But she wouldn't listen. She got mad.' She wiped her tears again. 'Then she took Barney and said she was gonna hide him.'

'Why haven't you told us this before?' Catherine asked.

'You wouldn't believe me. You say it's rubbish.' She looked up at Adam. 'Aunty Emma saw her in my window but you didn't believe that.'

'Bella, you have to tell us if something is upsetting you, okay? Even if you think me and your dad won't believe you, we will listen. You can't hide in your room when you get upset. This is no good, is it?'

'Can I sleep in your bed?' She hugged her mum tightly.

'Of course you can.' Catherine looked up at Adam. 'She'll fit in the middle of us.'

Suddenly they all looked out to the landing. They all heard it. There was no denying what it was, and this time there was no blaming Bella as she was sitting in between them. The footsteps started at Bella's door and seemed to run along the landing to the stairs, and then down the stairs to the bottom where they stopped. Adam got up and looked out onto the landing and across to the top of the stairs. There was nothing there. He looked back at his family. Catherine's eyes were wide, but Bella didn't look scared.

'That's Charlotte. She wants to play.'

'I'll go downstairs; I'll have a look.' Although he didn't believe in the paranormal Adam couldn't deny that his heart was pounding in his chest, the beat echoing in his head. He had no logical explanations as to what could have made that noise or how. He crept along the landing and looked down the stairs with anticipation. The light from the landing ended two-thirds of the way down the stairs, beyond was complete darkness. He had to go down. His legs were like jelly and he had to force them to move.

He took each step slowly, one by one. At the bottom he reached for the switch, which was on the left before the kitchen. His hand fumbled about on the wall but he couldn't find it. The longer it took, the more he began to panic. Eventually his fingers glided over it and he flicked it on. He looked around and didn't see anything. Then an object caught his eye: it was Barney by the front door.

'Well, I found Barney,' he said as he walked back into Bella's room, 'but I'm not sure how he could have made so much noise.' Bella took Barney back in her arms and held him close.

'Why don't we all go to bed, hmm? Together,' Catherine suggested. 'I think the three of us will be nice and toasty, won't we, Bella?'

'Yes, Mummy.' She seemed a lot happier now she was reunited with Barney. 'Am I going in the middle?'

'Yes, you are,' Adam said. 'That's your spot. But no pushing me out again. My shoulder has never been the same since.'

'Ha-ha. Okay, Daddy.'

They walked across the landing into Catherine and Adam's room and climbed into bed. Adam made sure the door was shut but left the landing light on in case Bella or Catherine needed to get up. Once they were all tucked in, Barney included, they tried to go to sleep. Bella went straight off, but Adam and Catherine had too many things on their minds. Charlotte?

CHAPTER 18

When the alarm went off in the morning neither Adam nor Catherine wanted to get up. They had barely slept due to the activities of the night before. There were no more disturbances after they got into bed but every noise they heard, owls hooting and foxes crying out, kept them on edge. Bella had no problems falling asleep. She was safely tucked up between her mum and dad.

Catherine reached over and turned off her painfully loud alarm. She rubbed her eyes which hurt from being so tired. Adam yawned and stretched, cracking his fingers as he tried to bring himself around. Catherine rolled over and let her bare feet touch the cold hardwood floor.

Bella didn't stir.

'Let her stay there for a bit longer,' Adam said. 'I'll drive her to school later. Let her have a lie in.'

They made their way downstairs. The house was quiet but light, as the sun shone bright through the gaps in the kitchen blinds.

'Did you put that there?' Catherine asked, looking at the floor. It was the folder they kept on a shelf in the kitchen containing all the documents given to them on the day of completion. It was now lying on the kitchen tiles with its paperwork falling out.

'There must be a draught from somewhere which blew it off,' Adam said. 'No other reason for it to fall. There's nothing else on the shelf to knock it.' He looked at the shelf but couldn't tell where a draught might have come from. It was nowhere near the window.

'This whole Charlotte thing,' Catherine said as she filled the kettle. 'What are we going to do?'

'What do you mean?'

'Do we bring someone in or what?'

'Look, we don't know for sure what's happened.' Adam got two cups from the cupboard and handed them to Catherine. 'We've never actually seen anything. If there is a little girl spirit running around the house, she isn't causing any of us any harm. I'd be concerned if it was Freddy Krueger but she sounds harmless.'

'But Bella was so heartbroken last night.'

'Yes, but that was because she was keeping it a secret. Now she knows she can speak to us about it, include us in it, she should be fine. She's not hurt, and she said she doesn't always see her. I think she'll be okay. I can't say I ever imagined believing in something like this, but I have to accept it. I don't think I'll be telling the guys at work, though.'

Catherine made them both a cup of coffee, they needed the caffeine, and they sat together in silence at the table until it was time to take Bella to school.

'Are you coming with us?' Adam asked as he stood up.

'No, I'll stay here, I think. Will you nip to the supermarket if I give you a list?'

'Course I will. Are you sure you won't come? I mean, will you be okay on your own?'

'I'll be fine. Like you said, it's not like this Charlotte is causing us any harm. She might only come out at night anyway, and if she was up as late as we were last night she'll need some sleep too!'

'Right.' He finished his coffee in one, big mouthful. 'I'll go get madam up, get dressed and then we can go. I'll let you write that list.'

He went upstairs leaving Catherine alone in the kitchen. She looked around and found that she didn't feel scared at all. She thought about Charlotte. If it was the same girl who lived here a hundred years ago, why would she be haunting the house? Her mother had run away with her and the other children and the farmhand, so why would she come back as a child?

As Catherine surveyed the kitchen she looked at the cupboards and remembered what her mother had said about there probably being muck on the top of them. She knew not to take her mother's words too seriously, but the house had been empty for some time before they moved in. There could be anything on top of there. It wouldn't hurt to get a ladder and give it a good clean.

Before Adam left with Bella he fetched the step ladder from the shed for Catherine, checking it for spiders first before he brought it into the house. She might be able to cope with a ghost, but she would definitely panic if there was a spider involved.

When Catherine climbed the ladder and investigated the tops of the cupboards she was surprised to find that they were not nearly as bad as she imagined they would be. There was a light layer of black dust but nothing major. She gave them a wipe down, carefully walking along the kitchen counter, working her way around.

She only just spotted it. Behind one of the cupboards there was what looked like the corner of a brown envelope, which had fallen down the back. It was being held up by an old cobweb. The spider was long gone so Catherine had no apprehension about pulling the envelope out. It was very old. The writing on the front had faded and was illegible. She climbed down off the kitchen counter and took it to the dining table to examine further. She pulled out three black-and-white photos.

The first photo showed a young man and woman. It must have been a wedding photo. Her dress was simple but white and she held a handful of flowers. He stood next to her looking very smart in a suit. He was an incredibly handsome young man and they looked very good together. It wasn't common for people to smile in old photos, Catherine knew, but something about them looked happy. On the back was a message: Henry and Elizabeth, 2 June 1904.

The second photo showed the same man and woman looking older but just as attractive. Elizabeth was sitting down and Henry was standing next to her in an army uniform. On Elizabeth's lap was a young boy, no more than three. On one side of her was a young girl aged approximately seven or eight and standing beside Henry was another little girl, slightly older than the other. On the back, there was another message: Henry, Elizabeth and the children, 15 December 1915.

The final photo was a single portrait of Henry in his uniform, standing in front of a fireplace with his arm on the mantelpiece. Catherine presumed it was during the First World War due to the date on the back: 7 January 1916.

Catherine set them down on the table, putting them in date order. She studied the children for a while wondering if one of the girls was Charlotte. Suddenly she felt light-headed. She thought she'd been ill because of the stress of her mother's visit but as that was over she couldn't understand why she felt like this. She put her head in her hands and leant her elbows on the table for a few minutes hoping it would stop. She heard the door open and close. *He's back early*, she thought. When Adam didn't come into the kitchen she decided to investigate, to see what he was doing. She was surprised, when she got to the kitchen doorway, to see a young girl standing at the bottom of the stairs. She was pretty and looked very familiar, like one of Bella's school friends.

'Where's Bella?' she asked.

'She's at school. Shouldn't you be there too? What's your name?'

The little girl laughed and ran up the stairs and towards Bella's room, her feet pounding.

'Wait, hang on!' Catherine went up after her, holding on to the banister as she was still feeling dizzy. 'Where have you gone?' She went into Bella's room but the little girl wasn't in there. 'Hello? Where are you?' She looked in all the rooms but couldn't find her. Could that have been Charlotte? She wished she had paid more attention to the little girl's face and clothes but with her head still spinning slightly it was difficult for her to focus. Back down the stairs, Catherine had to stop at the bottom and sit on the second to last step.

Adam walked through the door a moment later. 'I forgot my chuffing wallet! I'll go back out. What's the matter? Are you okay?' He sat down next to his wife and put his arm around her. 'Are you still feeling ill?'

'Yes, but… something strange just happened. I don't know if it was real or if I was imagining it with my head spinning like this, but she came in. The door opened and I thought it was you. I came out here and she was just standing there, so casually. I thought it was one of Bella's friends as she asked for her, but she ran upstairs and I lost her. And there's no one there. She looked so real.'

'A girl came in? Through the door?'

'Yes, opened and shut it. I heard it. She was stood at the bottom of the stairs when I came out.'

'What was she wearing?'

'I didn't notice.' She shook her head. 'I was too shocked at the time thinking I had a random girl running around the house and would have an angry mother out there somewhere. She looked so familiar–' she broke off. 'Oh, my God.' She got up and ran into the kitchen followed closely by a concerned Adam.

'What?' he asked.

She went to the table and picked up the black-and-white photo of the family all together. Adam looked over her shoulder. Catherine then pointed to the little girl on the right-hand side standing next to Elizabeth. The curly locks, the wide eyes, the cheeky expression.

'That was her. That was the little girl. That's Charlotte.'

CHAPTER 19

May 1916

*E*lizabeth sat at the table with a handful of letters from Henry. They had all been delivered together that morning. She read them over and over, hearing his voice in her head. She was very tired as she had not slept well again, thinking about what she had done. Her hair was loosely tied up with no care for her appearance and she was wearing an old, mucky apron. She picked up the letters again.

My dearest Elizabeth,

Today has been a hard day. We lost many men. There was nothing more I could do. It is the first time since being here that I have felt completely useless and a failure. Nothing that I did helped. They just kept coming. One after another, after another. The screams of men pierced my ears; I have never heard anything like it, and it hasn't stopped. Young boys fearing for their lives. I have been allowed a break and all I want is to speak to you. I wish I could hear your voice.

I must go back now. I will write again tomorrow. Pray for me. Pray for the other men.

Henry.

My dearest Elizabeth,

I have not slept. I don't know quite how long I have been awake. I remember waking up on Thursday morning. Today is Sunday but I do not know what time it is. They want to send me away for a couple of days, for a break. There is more fighting to come and they need me to recover and get ready. It is not long enough to come home but long enough to get away from here. I want to refuse; I cannot leave my men, but I have been ordered to go.

Henry.

My dearest Elizabeth,

I have had two days away and I am glad for it. I have slept and eaten and now I prepare to return. A few of your letters were handed to me this morning; they were redirected here, thank God. They have taken a while to get here judging by the postmark. I have read them over and over. That is excellent news about Toby and his speaking. You must teach him to say 'Daddy' for when I get home. Michael has clearly been a good influence. I am glad he has been spending time with you all. I feel better knowing there is someone watching over you all. I hope his father is well. I will do my best when I return. I am in debt to Michael now after all he is doing for us, so I will certainly return the favour for him. Such a good man.

Pass on my love to the children and my regards to Michael. I will see you all very soon.

We're halfway there now, my darling. Three months to go.

Keep on writing to me. Your letters are giving me the strength I need.

Henry.

It is as though he knows, Elizabeth thought, *either that or God has decided to punish me by making sure that these particular letters got delivered at the same time.* She had no words to put on the blank piece of paper in front of her. She tapped her pencil against the table: tap, tap, tap.

'Mum?' Mary startled her. 'You've broken it.'

'Sorry?'

'The pencil, it's snapped.'

She hadn't even noticed that it had snapped in two. She was in a world of her own remembering what had happened between her and Michael. About how she had let Henry down, let her children down and disgraced herself. There were no excuses. She had given in to desire and temptation and now she would have to confess to her husband.

She debated telling him by letter, but she knew it would destroy him with three more months left away from home. It was not the right way to confess. She would have to wait until he got home, but what could she say to him now? She picked up a new pencil and began to write:

Henry,

I am sorry you have been suffering. I cannot imagine the nightmare you are facing each day. I wish...

She screwed this up and started again.

My dearest Henry,

I wish I could send you words of comfort as you face the horrors that you do. I know you do not tell me everything that happens...

She screwed this up too and had to hold back tears of frustration.

My dearest husband,

I long for you to be home with us again soon. The children miss you terribly and I have been very lonely. I am glad you could have a break; I only wish it was long enough for you to come home. Even for a day.

We have three months left, as you say, we have almost made it. Stay strong. I will write to you as often as I can.

All my love,

your Elizabeth.

She put down the pencil and covered her face with her hands. She had never found it so hard before to write to her husband, her soulmate. She forgot that Mary was in the kitchen with her, watching her every move.

'What's happened, Mum?' she asked.

'What do you mean?'

'What's happened to Dad? Something has happened, hasn't it? I can tell you're upset. Is he okay?'

'Oh, Mary, no, nothing has happened. I'm sorry. He has been finding it tough but he's okay. It won't be long until he's home. I think we all want him back with us now. Don't we?'

They were disturbed by a knock on the door. A familiar knock.

'I'll get it!' Charlotte shouted from the living room. She ran to the door with Toby not far behind her. Elizabeth heard the door open and little Toby's excited voice.

'Michael!' he shouted. 'Michael, Michael, Mummy, Michael.' He ran to Elizabeth in the kitchen.

Michael walked into the kitchen slowly. It was his first time returning to the house since the night he spent with Elizabeth so he was not sure what kind of reception he would get. He could rely on Charlotte and Toby to be excited to see him. Maybe not Elizabeth today, certainly not Mary. Maybe Mary knew something like this would happen, he thought, maybe she knew not to trust him with her mother.

'Michael.' Elizabeth stood up. 'We didn't have any plans for you today. What are you doing here?'

It was so unusual for her to speak to him so formally. He was used to her being friendly and welcoming. He looked into her eyes longing for her to look back at him with the love and care she had previously, but there was nothing. Michael had no feelings of regret; he was glad that it had happened. His only regret was that Elizabeth was already married.

'I, erm.' He pulled his hat from his head and held it in both hands. 'I just…' He didn't know what to say, or why he had come in the first place. He couldn't say what he wanted to say in front of the children. 'I just wondered if you needed my help with anything today.'

'No, we have everything under control today, Michael. Thank you anyway.'

She could see the heartbreak in his face, but there was nothing else she could do. She couldn't have him in her house anymore; they had crossed the line. She needed to get him out of her life.

'He needs to come to the show tonight, Mummy,' Charlotte said. 'Michael, you need to come.'

'Charlotte, he doesn't want to go to the school.'

'What's happening at the school?' he asked Charlotte.

'I'm singing. I'm in the choir. We're doing a show. You have to come. I want you to come.'

'Well, if you really want me to.' He looked from Charlotte to Elizabeth. 'It will be a good distraction for me, with my father and all. I can sit at the back away from you all.'

Elizabeth felt yet more guilt. She had forgotten about his father dying.

'Of course you should come, I'm sorry. My mind is all over the place today and I completely forgot about your father. You can meet us there at seven o'clock. We will sit together.'

'That would be wonderful, thank you. I'll meet you there.' He put his hat back on his head. 'See you later, children. I'll see you all tonight.'

She sat back down to her letter to add a note to the end:

PS:

Michael's father died before I got a chance to offer him any help. He seemed to go peacefully in the end despite years of suffering. The house is in a terrible state. Michael will need someone in, to help him sort it out.

Mary and Charlotte are singing in the school choir tonight. It is to raise money for the families of soldiers who have been killed in action. Michael will be accompanying us by the request of Charlotte.

She put the finished letter in an envelope and sent Mary to the post office with it, with money for postage. Then she sent Charlotte and Toby upstairs to play together so she could have a few minutes of peace to reflect on the mess she was in.

CHAPTER 20

*M*ichael arrived early to the school hall. He watched children go in with their mothers as well as families of deceased soldiers. There were mothers and young wives wearing black armbands. He wondered if he had known or served with any of their sons and husbands. They saw him with his wooden leg and some came to give him their love and sympathy.

'Such bravery,' one lady said.

'God was looking down on you that day. You might have lost your leg, but you have your life,' said another.

'God bless you,' said a widowed woman who looked younger than him.

A few moments later he saw Elizabeth. She was carrying Toby and the girls were wearing their best dresses and walking alongside her. Elizabeth had made herself look presentable and Michael couldn't take his eyes off her.

'Hello, Michael. It was good of you to come,' she said. She sounded sincere but she was not smiling. 'Girls, you'd best go inside and get ready. We'll find our seats.'

The girls went inside. Elizabeth didn't seem to want to be

alone with Michael for too long and followed soon after the girls. They walked in together and were approached by the headmaster, Mr Stubbs. He had gone to school with Henry and so knew Elizabeth quite well.

'Elizabeth, it is good to see you.' They had not seen each other much since Henry left for training the year before. 'And this must be Michael, who we hear so much about from Charlotte.' They shook hands.

'It's a pleasure to meet you, sir.'

'The pleasure is all mine. I am glad you could come.' He looked at Michael's leg. 'Does it bring you much pain?'

'Not so much now, thank God. I stopped using my stick. It aches at times, but I was one of the lucky ones.'

'Yes, you were, my lad. Welcome home. Take your seats won't you, before it fills up. We'll be starting soon. I will come see you after, Elizabeth.'

They found some seats together near the back. Elizabeth kept a sleepy Toby on her lap.

'Why hasn't Mr Stubbs been called up?' Michael asked, trying to make conversation.

'He has a curved spine. He failed the medical.' Elizabeth answered swiftly before returning her gaze to her children who were now making their way on stage.

'We need to talk,' Michael said to her, quietly.

'Not now. And not here.' She looked around. 'There are too many people here, I don't want any rumours to start. But you need to stay away. Away from the house, the children, just away. We need to put some distance between us now. We'll talk another time.'

Michael had expected her to say this, but it still hurt to hear it. He didn't want to stay away. He wanted her, all of her, for himself. He didn't want to lose her.

After the show the children were given biscuits whilst the adults were offered tea or coffee. Toby took a biscuit and stayed on the chair eating it, slowly. Mary and Charlotte were talking with their friends. This left Michael and Elizabeth alone together. They stood in awkward silence. Neither of them knew what to say to each other. Michael wanted to beg and plead with Elizabeth not to keep him away.

'So, Michael, how have things been since you got back?' Mr Stubbs joined them both. 'Have you been able to find any work? I imagine it will be very difficult.'

'There isn't any work for me that I can do really. I can't work in the mills, and farmers take one look at me and laugh. They take pity on me, of course, but they need someone who can work fast and carry heavy loads and I just can't do that at the moment. I have been lucky.' He looked at Elizabeth. 'I met Henry in France and he introduced me to his family. I have been doing jobs for them. Elizabeth has been very kind. I don't know what I would have done without her.'

'Elizabeth is a saint,' Mr Stubbs said. Elizabeth blushed. 'If you're needing some work, young man, our caretaker is about to retire in a few weeks, well, at the end of the school year. Why don't you come and work at the school?'

'Oh, Mr Stubbs,' Elizabeth interjected. 'I'm not sure if he's ready for that yet. It will be such long days.'

'Nonsense. He will open the building up at seven thirty and then close it again for four o'clock. There will be odd jobs through the day as and when we need him. And the occasional evening event, of course, like today. But it's a simple enough job, I see no reason why he can't do it. And it will pay too. What do you say, Michael?'

'That... that would be good. Thank you.'

'Excellent! It's settled. Why don't you come back on the first of June? Mr Johnson can show you the ropes and you can take over when he goes.'

'I'll be there, thank you. That really means a lot.'

'My pleasure. Elizabeth, it has been good to see you. Come by sometime; Julie has been anxious to catch up with you.'

He walked away and they went back to silence.

'I think it is time we left. Mary–' Elizabeth called over to her daughter and put down her cup. '–get Charlotte, it's time we were going.'

'When can I see you?'

'I don't know. Not for a while. Please, leave me be, Michael. Just for a while.'

She picked up Toby who was now very sleepy and ready for bed. The girls followed as she rushed out of the door, and they went home leaving Michael on his own.

Michael watched her leave and decided he had to get her while she was alone. He *had* to speak to her.

CHAPTER 21

A week had passed since the choir's performance at the school. Elizabeth had not heard from Michael and had hoped he had decided to stay away. It could not happen again. She knew his father's funeral had taken place, as she had received a visit from the vicar the day before.

'Michael was alone at the funeral,' he said. 'I was surprised to not see you there. I think he would have benefited from some support.' The vicar was an elderly man. He had been at that church for over fifty years and had known Elizabeth's parents and her grandfather. 'Have you seen much of him lately?'

'No, Father, I haven't.' She wanted to confess to him what had happened but she was too ashamed. She wasn't ready yet. 'We have all been busy. And I don't want people to get the wrong impression of us.'

'No one thinks badly of your friendship. You are doing him a kindness.' His voice was soft and soothing. 'He spoke so highly of you at the funeral, and he dotes on your children. When these men return from war, there is no help for them, no therapy. What you're doing is therapy. You are helping him to recover.

And from what I understand, it has worked. He is to start working at the school soon, I hear.'

'Yes, he met Mr Stubbs last week and was offered the job of caretaker when Mr Johnson leaves.'

'It's good that he has that to fall back on. When they come back with a missing arm or leg there are no opportunities for them. They go to waste. I was worried he would go the same way as his father, but he is a bright young man. I remember him as a boy; he was so quiet and shy. You'd never know he was in the same room as you. But now he speaks with confidence and that's all down to you.'

Elizabeth did not want to take credit, but she knew he was right. Michael had certainly come out of his shell these last couple of months and it was because of her. She had led him on, she realised. She blamed herself for what had happened.

It was a warm Wednesday morning on the last day of May. The older children were at school and Toby was having a nap. He had been poorly the night before and so had not slept much. Elizabeth had put him back to bed after he had lunch. When she came downstairs, she saw the postman walking down the garden path and went out to meet him.

'Good morning, Mrs Jones. Beautiful day.'

'Good morning, Tom. It is lovely today.'

'Another one from France.' He handed her the letter. 'Send him my best, won't you? Tell him we all miss him.'

'Of course. Take care.'

She took the letter inside and made herself a pot of tea before opening it. She got a pencil and some paper ready to reply straight away.

My dearest Elizabeth,

I have been sent to work in a hospital in the north. I am glad of the change of scenery. I am not sure how long I will be here but am glad to be out of that place. I have been given some clean uniform, which is a blessing. I never truly appreciated clean, dry socks! Although ever since I got here the weather has picked up. How typical. Whilst I am outside in the trenches it pours with rain; now I am working inside, the sun is shining. Funny how that happens, isn't it?

I still have some time before I return to work so I will have a nap. I wanted to write you a quick note so you knew I was fine. I don't want you worrying after my last letters.

All my love,

Henry.

Elizabeth was pleased how much Henry's mood had picked up. She had certainly been worried after his last letters; he was right about that. She started to write back when there was a knock at the door. Perhaps the postman had forgotten something. She put the pencil down and walked to the door.

'Michael,' she said, as he stood in the doorway. 'What are you doing here?'

'I know the girls are in school now. I have to speak to you.'

'Michael, it's not a good time. I have so much work to do.'

'Then let me help. Nothing has changed. I can still lend a hand around the house. Let me help, Elizabeth.'

'Come in.' She didn't want to argue with him on the doorstep where anyone could overhear. 'Look, Michael, I have nothing to say. What happened, it was a mistake.'

'Don't say that.' He stepped towards her and went to stroke her cheek but she pulled away. 'Don't be like that. Please, Elizabeth.'

'You can't come around here anymore. What we did was wrong. Henry doesn't deserve this, and he will be home soon. The sooner the better. I'll have to tell him.'

'You can't tell him, he'll hate me.'

'Yes, of course he will. He'll hate us both and he'll have every right to, but I can't lie to him. He's a good man, and I have failed him as a wife.' It was the first she had spoken about it out loud. 'I am a disgusting woman and I don't deserve a man like Henry.'

'You're not disgusting.' He reached out to stroke her face again and this time she didn't pull away. She allowed him to wipe the warm tears off her cheeks.

He felt sorry for her, and for how much it would hurt Henry to know the truth. But if the war had taught him anything, it was to live in the moment as you never knew when your time was up.

'You are an amazing woman, a wonderful mother.' He moved closer to her. 'And you're beautiful. I wish you weren't married, and then I would take you away from here to be with me.' He held her face with both hands, tears filling his eyes. 'You are the woman I want to spend my life with. I've hated not seeing you every day. It pains me that you are just a walk away and I cannot come to you. I need you, Elizabeth. I could have died, but God spared me and sent me to you. Don't you see that?'

'Michael…' She looked into his eyes. 'You can't…'

'What?' His face moved closer to hers, their noses almost touching. 'Can't what?' he whispered, as their lips nearly met.

'Mummy?' Toby shouted from his bedroom. He was crying. Michael and Elizabeth jumped apart.

'Toby, he's been poorly. I should have checked on him.' She rushed past Michael and he grabbed her arm.

'I'll be right here.'

She half smiled and hurried upstairs. It took half an hour to settle Toby down. He had a high fever but eventually fell back to sleep. Elizabeth did all she could, but she knew he mostly needed to rest. She went back downstairs to join Michael.

'He's asleep.'

'Good. Is there anything I can do?'

'No, the girls will be home soon.'

'Do you want me to go?' he asked.

Elizabeth thought about this. It would be best if he left but, to be truthful, she wanted him to stay.

'No, you should stay for dinner. You can tell me about your father's funeral. I should have been there for you.'

When the girls came home they all had dinner together. Toby joined them as he felt well enough to come down to eat, but once his tummy was full of hot food he was ready to go back to sleep. Michael put him to bed whilst Elizabeth tidied up. Mary helped Charlotte with some homework and soon they went off to bed too. It left Michael and Elizabeth on the sofa together. They sat in silence until it was time for Michael to go.

'Are you all set for your first day tomorrow?' Elizabeth said.

'I am. Well, kind of. I don't know what I'll need to take with me. Mr Stubbs didn't really give me much information.'

'Well, you'll need to take some sandwiches for lunch and make sure you have something suitable to wear. Have you got either of those sorted?'

'Erm, no. I only have the clothes I'm wearing now, and as for sandwiches, I've never been skilled in anything but slicing bread.'

'Oh, Michael. What am I going to do with you? Wait there.' Michael stayed in the living room whilst Elizabeth went upstairs. She came back down with some overalls.

'Try these on,' she instructed. 'Make sure they fit. If not, I still have some time to alter them. I'll go make you up a sandwich for tomorrow while you pop them on.'

'Thank you. You don't have to do this.'

'Yes, I do. You'll need a good lunch if you're starting work early tomorrow. Try them on in here and I'll be in the kitchen.'

In the kitchen, she cut up some thick slices of freshly baked bread and filled them with ham and homemade mayonnaise before wrapping the sandwich in a napkin so it was ready for him to take away.

'They're perfect; they fit really well.' Michael walked into the kitchen wearing the overalls. 'Are you sure Henry won't mind?'

'I think you wearing his clothes will be the least of his worries, if I'm honest. Here, I made you a sandwich. Come back tomorrow night if you need another for Friday.'

'Thank you.' She tried to wave him away saying it was nothing. 'No, seriously. Elizabeth, thank you. I know you wanted me to stay away but I can't help myself. I can't stay away from you.' He reached for her hands.

'Michael, the children are upstairs. I can't...'

'Shh, don't speak. I'm done speaking now. Let me be with you.'

'Michael...'

'Shhh.'

CHAPTER 22

May 2016

'*H*ow was your night? Did anything happen?' Adam asked when he got home from work. It was a little after midnight and the house was silent. 'Is Bella okay?'

'We're all fine. Nothing has happened all night.' Catherine was still at the kitchen table working on some new cake designs and had not realised what the time was. 'Bella wanted to play in the garden earlier.'

'Did you let her?'

'No, how could I? It's all so overgrown.' The front garden had been kept tidy and presentable, but the same could not be said for the back. It had been neglected badly over the last few decades. 'We really need to do something to it. Get it all cut back, pull out the weeds, tidy it up. We might need to get someone in to do it; it's a bloody big garden. What do you think?'

'Well, you did promise Emma a barbeque party in the summer.' He raised his eyebrows in disapproval. 'But we don't need to bring anyone in for it. I can handle it. I'm off all weekend, I'll get it done.'

'Really?'

'Well, most of it. There are some tools in the shed, I think, left by the previous owners. I'm sure Bella will want to lend a hand.'

'Oh yes, I'm sure she'll be a great help when she spots a butterfly and tries to fly away with it, leaving you on your own.'

Adam brought them both a cup of tea and sat at the table with her.

'Just let me have a little sleep in tomorrow, but I'll try to get up mid-morning and then I can be out most of the day. What do you have planned?'

'Nothing really. I don't have any cakes booked in for a couple of weeks so I can help out.' She closed her design book and sipped her cup of tea realising how tired she actually was.

'You know, if we clear some space out, we can get some equipment for Bella. Like a slide and swings and stuff. If we get it done in time for her birthday, she can have a little party,' Adam suggested.

'Aw, yes, that's a brilliant idea. I was going to arrange something at Dory's Corner for her, but I prefer that idea. We have a month to get it done then.'

'Not a problem.'

The next morning, Adam got up as he had promised and headed out to the shed with Bella in tow in search of spades and any other tools he could find. He had bin bags ready to collect any unwanted plant life. Bella had her wellies on ready, and was excited to get muddy. The sun was shining and there wasn't a cloud in sight. Catherine made sure Bella was wearing some sun cream to prevent her from burning in the heat. She joined them too but would not be getting muddy and would be staying far away from any potential spiders.

In the shed Adam was surprised to find a hand fork, rakes and shears. They looked unused.

'Bella, why don't you bring me that thing there shaped like a big fork, and I'll carry these big garden scissors. Have you got it?'

'Yes, Daddy. What are you going to cut with them?'

'Well, you know how Mummy said you couldn't play in the garden yesterday?' She nodded at him. 'It's because the grass and weeds have become so overgrown, we're not sure if there's an ogre living in there or not.'

'Daddy!' She laughed. 'Ogres aren't real!'

'Of course they are! Big green creatures. And they're not friendly like Shrek. Oh no. So we have to dig them out of their dens and banish them from the garden.'

'Don't scare her!' Catherine called across to them when she overheard. 'She'll be having nightmares.'

'Well, then we need to make sure our garden is ogre-free, don't we, Bella?'

'Yes, Daddy!' she said. 'Let's dig!'

Adam looked across the garden. He hadn't noticed how big it was until now. He had seen the boundary on the deeds of the property but it looked much bigger in reality. He knew it would take longer than the weekend to get it completed but would do what he could.

The sun was high in the sky, burning down on them, but by late afternoon they had done an awful lot of work. Bella kept to the shade pulling out the smaller weeds and putting them in her own bag. Adam set about cutting back the overgrown bushes and trees. There were weeds, now as big as small trees, which would not pull out easily. Catherine was on hand to assist, although her hay fever was making it tricky.

'Have you not taken anything for it?' Adam asked, seeing his wife's eyes streaming with tears. 'Why don't you go inside?'

'It's not too bad,' she said, sniffling. 'I took something earlier.' She wiped her eyes and then blew her nose on a tissue she had in her pocket. 'There, much better. I can see now. Adam, what's that?'

'What?' He looked into the trees assuming she had seen a mouse or other animal.

'No, not there, in the house.' She pointed. 'Our bedroom window.'

He looked up and saw it instantly. The face. A woman's face. A woman was looking down at them. Watching them. Her hand was pressed against the window and her eyes were fixed on theirs. Adam and Catherine both froze. Bella was singing to herself as she pulled dandelions out of the grass, not paying attention. But they could not move their eyes away from the woman. The woman's face turned towards Bella and then back towards them.

'What is she saying?' Adam asked quietly. He could hear his heart beating in his chest. 'Her lips are moving.'

Catherine watched as the woman tried to speak to them. Her eyes looked sad and teary. She was clearly crying.

'It's Elizabeth. I need to go up.' Catherine stepped forward.

'Don't go up!' Adam grabbed her arm and pulled her to face him. 'Are you mad?'

'She's trying to tell us something,' she whispered. 'We need to know why they're here. Don't you want to know?'

'Not right now, I don't.' He nodded his head towards Bella. 'If she's in our room we'll try find her later when madam is asleep, okay?'

'Okay,' Catherine agreed. She looked at Bella who hadn't noticed what was going on, then back up at the house. 'Where has she gone?'

Elizabeth had vanished. A condensation mark was quickly disappearing from where her hand had been pressed.

'Let's just carry on with the garden, okay?' Adam looked at his watch. 'It's only four o'clock. Just another hour and we can leave it till the morning. Sound good?'

'Yeah.' Catherine was still staring at the house, at every window, searching for movement. 'Yeah, sounds good.'

They continued working for just under an hour before Bella said she was tired and wanted to go in. The garden was beginning to look bigger already. There were twelve bags filled with garden waste and piles of other rubbish which needed to be taken away. They were proud of how much they had done.

'Not bad, eh, chaps?' Adam said. 'Tomorrow though, guys, if you could put a little more effort in so I'm not doing it all myself, yeah?' He laughed.

Catherine hit him on the arm. 'Don't even joke about it, you. I said we should get someone in but, "oh no I'll do it myself",' she mocked him. 'So now, guess what? You can do it all yourself. Oh no, don't!' Adam pulled her in for a kiss. 'No, you're all sweaty!'

'Yeah and you love it. Don't pretend like you don't.'

'Eww, Daddy, you're all muddy.' Bella laughed at her parents' playfulness.

They walked through the back doorway into the kitchen leaving their muddy shoes and tools at the door. Then took it in turns to wash their hands. Catherine poured them all some cold lemonade.

'Mummy, why is that on the floor?' Bella pointed to the folder of paperwork.

'Why does that keep making its way to the floor?' Catherine picked it up and began putting all the paperwork back inside when she noticed the newspaper articles. She pulled them out and put them on the table.

'What are they?' Adam asked.

'They're newspaper cuttings. I hadn't bothered reading them before. Look at the date: 12 September 1916.'

LOCAL FAMILY REPORTED MISSING

The young family, residing at Abberton House, were reported missing last month by husband and father Dr Henry Jones when he returned on leave from fighting in France. The mystery of their disappearance remains unsolved as there are no clues to their whereabouts. It is believed they fled sometime during the night leaving all their personal belongings behind. Some villagers report that Mrs Jones was having an affair with local resident Pte Michael Staines who has also been reported missing. Staines, who served in France alongside Dr Jones, had been sent home early following an injury. Dr Jones says he'd put his trust in Staines to watch over his family until he was able to return last month. He is fearful for his wife and children's safety. Local police are now searching for Staines, who may be suffering from bouts of mental instability after his time in France. Enquiries are ongoing.

There was a photo beneath the article, the same one showing the family that Catherine had found on top of the cupboards. Each member was named beneath it: Henry, Elizabeth, Mary, Charlotte and Toby.

Another article.

2 November 1916

Investigations into the disappearance of the Jones family have been cancelled due to lack of evidence. Officers now believe Staines was having improper relations with Mrs Jones and that they left together with the children. Staines' recently deceased father had family residing in Scotland. It is thought that this is where they headed.

Dr Jones failed to return to duty in France. His mental state is now under observation.

'Well, that certainly paints a picture.'

'Doesn't it just.' Catherine put the clippings down on the table. 'I wonder if there are any more.'

She pulled everything out of the folder and found one more article. This one was written by a local reporter focusing on Henry after the war.

2 June 1922

Dr Henry Jones served only six months abroad in 1916. He returned home in August of that year to spend a few weeks' leave with his family; however, his world was turned upside down when he discovered they had disappeared. He reported to the police that he first became worried when he stopped receiving letters from his wife in June 1916. His superiors told him that it was normal for post to go astray in times of war.

He raised the alarm on 12 August 1916 when his family were not home to welcome him. Their beds were made and empty. Food was on the stove, uneaten. There was no sign of them. Dr Jones states he ran to neighbouring houses and to an elderly aunt's house nearby, but no one had seen them. He was then told of suspicions of his wife having an affair with a young man she had befriended. He was at the house regularly, late into the night, sometimes not leaving until morning.

Dr Jones would not accept this and turned into a changed man. Once the much-loved village doctor, he became a recluse. He shunned visitors and was soon discharged from the army due to ill health.

He has now returned to his medical duties in the village; however, he refuses to accept the truth: Mrs Jones made her choice. He still stands by the belief that she did not leave, but that she and the children have been taken from him. One day, he will accept the truth, but for now he is looked upon with pity for being so foolish.

'How awful is that?' Adam asked. 'Poor man.'

'Well, they were hardly going to sympathise with him, were they? He was searching for a woman who had an affair. It's not like modern-day "let's go on Jeremy Kyle". That was really bad, back then. Shameful. And in a village as small as this, can you imagine the gossip?'

'Wait, what's that one?'

'What?'

'There, here.' Adam pulled out a more recent looking slip of newspaper.

12 May 1966

Death notifications

Dr Henry Jones, aged 80, owner of Abberton House and surrounding land, was found dead on the eighth of May near the front door of the property by a neighbour. Land and estate are to be passed on to a distant relative in Australia.

'Look at the photo.'

There was a black-and-white photo showing an elderly man whom Adam and Catherine instantly recognised as the man who had been visiting their house, looking for his family.

CHAPTER 23

*S*aturday night was uneventful despite their sightings in the afternoon. Adam and Catherine found themselves avoiding going to bed for as long as possible. Earlier, Catherine had had no fear of going up to their room to speak to Elizabeth, but now darkness had set in she felt different. Bella fell asleep as soon as she had eaten her tea after the long, hard day of work; however, her parents were fighting their fatigued state, which tired them out even more.

'Come on,' Adam said, whilst yawning, 'let's stop being silly now. It's almost midnight and I want to get back out in that garden first thing. Martin said he'd be here about four o'clock with the van, so we need to bag up as much crap as possible by then.' He heaved himself off the couch and helped to pull Catherine up too.

Up in their room there was no sign of Elizabeth and they managed to have a peaceful night's sleep. They were woken in the morning by Bella who was excited to get back out in the garden.

'Have you seen Charlotte lately, Bella?' Catherine asked as they ate breakfast.

'No, Mummy. I don't know where she's gone. It's been ages.'

Bella took a final mouthful of Weetabix and finished her glass of chocolate milk. 'I'm ready, Daddy!'

'Come on then, flower. Let's see if we have more luck finding that ogre today.'

Catherine looked out the window to check on the weather. It was very gloomy compared to the day before. The sun was hidden by thick grey clouds and there was a slight fog over the bottom of their garden.

'That'll clear in no time,' Adam insisted. 'Bella, don't disappear too far down, okay? I won't be able to see you until it clears.'

'Okay, Daddy.' She was already slipping into her wellies.

'Are you coming out too?' Adam asked Catherine.

'I'll come out for a bit, but I want to get stuff ready for tea. I want it to be right. God forbid we have crunchy roast potatoes again.'

'I happen to like my potatoes crunchy.' He kissed her on the lips.

'Eww, Daddy, that's gross!'

He turned to his daughter and quickly grabbed her before she could run away. She immediately started giggling thinking she was going to get tickled. Instead, Adam started planting kisses on her cheeks and head.

'"Gross" is it, madam?'

'Ha-ha! Daddy, stop!' she screeched. 'What about the ogre?'

'I'm not kissing an ogre.'

'No,' she said, laughing, 'we need to find the ogres. You said so!'

'Hmm, you're right.' He put her down. 'Go on then.' He opened the door. 'I'm right behind you. You get started.' Off she ran to the same spot she was working on yesterday.

'Oh, hang on, we need more bags.' Catherine remembered they had used the last one yesterday. She opened the cupboard under the sink and pulled out a new roll.

Then it started.

Heavy footsteps echoed above them, running from one end of the landing to the other. Back and forth. Back and forth.

'There's more than one,' Adam observed. They both listened closely.

'Are you sure?'

He listened carefully as the footsteps continued to run along the landing.

'Definitely.' He nodded his head. 'Yes, definitely. Can't you hear it? One of them sets off and the other follows just after. They're a little bit lighter than the first.' They stood quietly to listen again. 'See?'

The steps came back along the landing but then started to make their way down the stairs. Adam and Catherine both jumped. They didn't know what was going to appear around the corner in just a few seconds. Down the footsteps came, each bang echoing in the hallway. They stopped suddenly on the bottom step but didn't go any further.

Adam and Catherine slowly walked to the kitchen doorway and looked out, tentatively, towards the stairs. There was nothing there. They both stepped out fully so they could check the whole staircase, but there was no one there.

'Mummy! Daddy! Where are you?' Bella shouted through the back door.

'We're coming,' they both shouted in unison, louder than intended, before walking back through the kitchen and out into the garden in silence.

The work in the garden went on without any disturbances from the house. Every now and then Catherine would sneak a glance at the windows to see if Elizabeth had returned, but there was no sign of her. As the day wore on, she eventually went inside to get started on dinner. In the afternoon, Martin arrived with the van and he and Adam moved the bags into the back so they could be taken to the household waste site before it closed.

When Catherine stepped out into the garden later, for the first time she was able to see its potential. She imagined getting a landscape gardener in to design and create a footpath which would lead to the bottom, where they could have a summer house big enough for a seating area as well as extra seating outside. There could be a barbeque nearby and there would still be plenty of room for Bella to have swings and a slide.

'We'll do what we can for now,' Adam said. 'We'll make it presentable, but I think our budget is a bit tight at the moment.'

Catherine knew he was right. The choice was either a perfectly manicured garden or getting the central heating fixed and added to the conservatory. They hadn't been in the conservatory at all apart from putting things in there for storage. But Catherine envisioned their first Christmas in the house taking place in there. There was enough room for a tree and a family-sized dining table. For the first time they would be able to host Christmas dinner for their families. Not that Catherine expected her own parents to make it, but she knew her sister would come.

'Bella, I think it's bedtime now,' Adam said as he saw her nodding off in the armchair. It was eight o'clock and she'd had another busy day in the garden. 'School tomorrow. You can tell everyone that we banished a great big ogre from the garden.'

Bella went up to bed, followed by Catherine who went to tuck her in. When Catherine came back down, she found Adam lying back on the couch with his eyes closed.

'I think it's bedtime for you too, mister. You've had a busy weekend.'

'You could be right.' He rubbed his eyes. 'Maybe an early one would be a good idea. Are the doors locked?'

'Yep, everything is done except the washing up, which can be finished tomorrow. Come on, let's go to bed.'

They were soon tucked up in bed as well and it wasn't long before they were both in a deep sleep.

Catherine woke up. It felt as though there was something fumbling on top of her, like a cat. She came around a bit more, slowly realising what was happening, but before she could do anything, a heavy force pushed down on her. The quilt was forced over her mouth and nose and her arms trapped. She couldn't move or breathe. She pushed as hard as she could against the pressure, but nothing would work. She was powerless. Suddenly the quilt loosened. It had only lasted seconds, but it felt much longer.

'Adam!' she cried out, fumbling for the lamp beside her, almost knocking it over. 'Adam!'

'What's up?' He rolled over and, in the light, he could see her face, which was red and flustered. 'Oh my God, what's happened?'

'I couldn't breathe,' Catherine cried. She began telling him what had happened, and then she spotted her in the corner. 'Adam...'

'Are you all right? Do you want anything?' He sat up to face her.

'Adam...'

'What is it?'

'Look...' She pointed behind him to the figure standing by the window. Adam turned. Seeing the woman standing there, he started, and pushed his back as far as he could into the headboard, throwing his arm in front of his wife to protect her.

There she stood. She wore a long brown skirt, a white blouse buttoned up to the neck with long sleeves. She had a pretty face but it was very pale, her hair loose around her shoulders. She looked at them, her lips moving but making no sound. She then looked to the window and put her hand on the glass through the curtains.

'Elizabeth?' Catherine said with a shaky voice.

This got her attention again, and she looked back at them. Her eyes were now wide and focused on Catherine. She uttered a word. They both listened carefully.

'It sounds like…' Adam said, thinking about what he had just heard. 'It sounds like "Henry".'

'No,' Catherine disagreed. She had heard something else. 'She's saying "help me". She wants our help.'

Suddenly Elizabeth fell to her knees, let out a loud cry and disappeared before them. She was gone but a cold chill remained in the air. Adam and Catherine sat in stunned silence, unable to move. For a moment neither believed it had actually happened, until red marks appeared on Catherine's face and arms from being held down.

'What did you say she'd said?' Adam asked as he relaxed his arm, finally able to speak.

'Help me. She said, "help me".'

CHAPTER 24

It was a long and sleepless night for both Catherine and Adam. Once they had taken Bella to school the next morning, they came straight home and fell asleep on the sofa. Neither of them were eager to go back to the bedroom just yet. They woke up at noon to the sound of the house phone ringing. Adam got up but was too late to answer it. He checked to see if a message had been left.

Catherine, Bridie here. How are you, my dear? I'm ringing to see if you could do another cake for me. My granddaughter will be sixteen next month and I know you will have some wonderful ideas. Give me a call as soon as you can. Goodbye.

'It was for you.' Adam put the phone back down. 'Birdy wants you to call her for another cake.' He yawned and stretched by the door.

'Oh, that's good. Her arm must still be broken.'

'Are you feeling okay after last night?'

'I'm fine. It didn't seem real. I just don't know why she'd do that to me.' She rubbed her hand against her mouth. 'Why would she try and suffocate me?'

'Maybe it was your snoring. I was half tempted myself, but she beat me to it.'

'You cheeky arse.' She threw a cushion across the room at him. 'It's not funny. What if they do it to Bella?'

'I know.' He sat back down on the couch next to Catherine. 'I think we need to ask her a bit more about what she's seen, and what Charlotte has said. Charlotte could be trying to pass on a message, but Bella doesn't understand.'

'Yes, but don't scare her though. We'll ask her tonight after school. Once she's had tea and settled. I don't want her knowing about last night.'

'Speaking of tea, what will we be having?'

'We need to go shopping. We don't have much in.'

'Okay, I'll nip out for something now and then you can call Birdy back to find out what she's wanting.'

'Yes, boss.' Catherine gave him a salute.

He kissed her on the cheek and put on his shoes. Once he was ready he picked up his keys and was off out the door. Catherine phoned Bridie back straight away and arranged for her to come by the next day to discuss what her granddaughter might like for a cake. She decided to get her design book out ready, so headed for her office.

Mary.

Catherine recognised her straight away from the black-and-white photo. She stood in Catherine's office by the table. She was as clear as day. Her green eyes looking straight at Catherine like she had been waiting for her.

'Mary?' Catherine said, softly. She was beginning to feel a little braver after everything that had happened in the house, although she was still scared at that very moment. It didn't feel real. 'Are you Mary?'

The girl nodded. Her head was tilted slightly to one side, her expression sad and deeply worried, like she had something to say. They stood in silence for what felt like hours to Catherine but could only have been a few seconds, not taking their eyes off each other. Catherine remembered what she and Adam had been talking about. It was now or never.

'Mary, what do you want?' Catherine's voice was shaking.

Mary seemed to take this in for a few minutes before she answered. As though speaking would take all the effort she had.

'You... almost... had it.' Her voice was quiet and delicate. Tears seemed to fill her eyes.

Catherine didn't know what Mary meant by that. Was she speaking to her directly or just saying words like Henry seemed to?

'Had what? What did we almost have?'

'You... just... missed.' She then inhaled a painful breath and as quickly as she had appeared, she was gone.

'Mary? Mary?' Catherine walked around the room, but Mary had gone. There was no sign of her anywhere.

CHAPTER 25

'It seems as though when they try to speak to us directly, it uses up all the energy or power they have, or whatever it is they use to appear,' Catherine said to Adam as they waited together outside Bella's school. They purposely stood away from the other parents so they could not be overheard.

'We're going to struggle to find out what they want from us if they can't actually speak to us.' Adam kept his voice low.

'We'll just have to keep trying. I don't want the situation to get any worse. I just can't get what Mary said out of my head.'

'"You just missed". What on earth does that mean? Missed what?'

'I've no idea. It's the first time Mary has made herself known. I wonder if she'll come back.'

'Catherine! Adam!' Gillian's voice called over. They looked and saw her making her way towards them. 'I've been waving at you for the last five minutes, but you were both in a world of your own, I think. I was starting to feel silly.'

'So sorry, Gillian. We didn't see you. We're a bit distracted at the moment.' Catherine forced a smile.

'Oh? What's the matter?'

'The garden.' Adam could sense she was fishing for some gossip, so he quickly jumped in. 'We're in the middle of doing the garden and just debating what we could plant, what we need to buy, that kind of thing.'

'Well,' she said excitedly, 'if you're looking for some help, my neighbour's husband is a landscape gardener. He would be brilliant. I'll get his number for you next time I see him.'

'Well actually…'

'That would be great, Gillian, thank you,' Catherine said. 'There's no rush, though. We might have to leave it until next year. How's Janey?'

'Janey is great, always talking about Bella. I think they'll be friends for life.' She smiled. 'I'm just struggling at the moment. Steven and I have been invited to a wedding in Kendal this weekend. We'll be staying over, so Janey was going to stay with my mother but she's been very poorly and is only just recovering. I don't want Janey to tire her out.'

'We can have her, if you like?' Catherine offered. 'Bella would love it.'

'Are you sure? That'd be great if you would.' She looked as though a weight had been lifted from her shoulders. 'They might drive you mad and keep you awake all night. I'd hate for you to lose sleep.'

'That won't be a problem for us,' Adam said, thinking over the recent nights of lost sleep. 'It'd be a pleasure to have her.'

'You have no idea how much that would help.' They all turned as they heard the school doors open. 'Here they come. I'll call you later, Catherine. Bye.'

'And what if our house guests make themselves known whilst Janey is in the house?' Adam asked when Gillian was a safe enough distance away to not overhear. 'Just because Bella isn't scared doesn't mean Janey won't be.'

'I didn't even think of that. I just know Bella would love it if her friend came over.'

'I'm sure it'll be fine. We'll just have to keep checking on them. Here she comes.' Adam held out his arms to catch his daughter who came running over to him. 'How you doing, flower? Have you had a good day?'

'Yeah, really good! Miss Arundale brought in her goldfish today and he's going to live in our class. He only has one eye.'

'Oh dear, that's no good is it?'

They all walked to the car. It was a quiet journey back, but as they were driving it only took a few minutes to reach the house. Once inside, they decided to tell Bella the exciting news.

'So, Bella,' Catherine started, as she handed Bella a glass of chocolate milk, 'we're going to have a house guest on Saturday. Can you guess who?'

'Aunty Emma? Is she coming back? She promised she would!'

'No, not Emma. She'll be here next month for your birthday, though. It's Janey. Janey will be sleeping over on Saturday night. Won't that be fun?'

'Really? Is she really? Yay, Mummy!' She ran to give Catherine a hug, spilling her milk as she did. 'I'm so excited she'll get to meet Barney and we can watch telly and we can play in the garden and–'

'There's lots you can do,' Adam said. 'You will have to speak to her tomorrow and ask her what she'd like to do when she comes over.'

'Yes. And ask her what she would like for tea and breakfast too. We can get fish and chips if she likes that. Don't forget to ask her tomorrow.'

'I won't, Mummy. I can't wait for Saturday.'

'Good, now go watch some telly whilst we get your tea ready. It won't be long.'

Bella took the rest of her drink into the living room. Adam helped Catherine get their tea ready whilst going over how they would broach the subject of Charlotte. They decided to keep it simple. They wanted to avoid scaring Bella and making her think there was something wrong. All they wanted to know was what Charlotte may have said to her to give them any more clues.

'Use your knife, Bella, not just the fork. You need to cut your fish fingers,' Adam instructed her as they all sat around the table, eating. Bella had picked up a whole fish finger with her fork and was attempting to eat it that way. 'Do you want me to show you how to do it?'

'No, Daddy, I can do it.' She picked up her knife and began to cut it up.

'So, Bella, your dad and I were talking earlier about Charlotte. Have you seen her lately?'

'No. I know she was in my room last night but I didn't see her.'

'How do you know she was there?'

'Because I had Barney in bed with me but when I woke up I couldn't find him. He was by the door. She is always taking Barney from me.' Bella took a bite of her food.

'How often have you spoken to her?' Adam asked, trying to be as casual as possible.

'A few times.' Bella swallowed her food. 'She likes to talk but she always wants to play.'

'And what has she said?' Bella looked up and saw her parents both looking at her, waiting for her answer.

'She talks about the garden. She wants me to go out with her, but always at night. I can't go out at night, can I?'

'Definitely not. We won't be happy if you go outside without telling us. Did she say why she wants you to go in the garden?'

'She just says Toby is out there. She wants to go get him. Like they're playing hide and seek and she needs to find him. But when I said I can't go out, she got mad. That's when you came in my room.'

'Why would she get mad?' Catherine asked. 'Can't he just come inside like she does?'

'I don't know.'

'Has she mentioned any of her family?'

'No.'

'Has she said anything else?'

'No.' Bella thought really hard about all the questions her mum and dad were asking. Charlotte wanted to play in her room, run around the landing and then go outside. It was always the same, and that's what Bella told them. She had nothing else to say.

'Okay. Well, good girl for eating all your food. Why don't you go back to watching telly and I'll bring you in a yoghurt in a little while.'

'Okay, Mummy.'

Bella went back into the living room.

'Well–' Adam got up from the table and carried all their plates to the sink. '–we didn't get much there. Just that Toby is in the garden. I wonder if that's why Elizabeth stands by the window. She's looking out for Toby.'

'We've never seen him though, have we?'

'We'd never seen Mary until you saw her today. Maybe he's too little for us to see, or not strong enough to make himself known. How old was he in the photo?'

'He looked about two years old, if that. Very young.'

Adam sat back down next to Catherine. 'I have to say, I'm starting to wonder if the family ran away with that young man at all. If they did, why would they be haunting the house at the age they are? Surely the kids should be older? There'd be no other reason for them being here at all unless...'

'Unless what?'

'Unless... they were killed.'

'Oh, Adam, that's awful. Who would do that to a whole family?'

'A madman, a shunned lover, or it could have been suicide?'

'But there were no bodies. Anything like that, they would have been found. Four bodies would be very difficult to hide.'

*J*aney was dropped off Saturday afternoon by both her parents who were all dressed up to go to the wedding. They kissed her goodbye and then drove away. Adam was working until later so Catherine decided to take both the girls to Dory's Corner for an hour, hoping it would help to tire them out before bedtime. Catherine had struggled to find time to take Bella there again and today would be a great opportunity. It was nice to see her daughter so happy spending time with Janey. They both laughed loudly as they competed with each other to get higher on the swings.

'Are you Catherine?' The owner of the café had come from behind the counter to join her at her table beside the window. Catherine guessed she was in her forties.

'Yes,' Catherine responded, wondering how she knew her name and why she was popping over to see her.

'I'm sorry to bother you. I won't keep you for long, but I wanted to ask you something.'

'Of course.'

'My name is Anne. My mother was Doreen, who opened the café many years ago. She died not so long back and I took over. I had the play area extended and made more secure too. It's so popular with the kids.'

'It's wonderful, Bella loves it. I only wish I could bring her more often.'

Anne smiled. 'That's wonderful to hear. Well, the reason I'm bothering you today is, my mother always had fresh cakes made to sell at the weekend. They went down really well with the passing tourists. Thing is, I'm not a baker. I've heard from my friend Bridie that you did a cake for her not so long ago.'

'Yes, and she's just booked me to do another one for her granddaughter.'

'She absolutely raved about the one you did for her grandson. She showed me photos and then your website. Your cakes are so creative and unique.'

'Aw, thank you. That's wonderful to hear too.'

'I'm coming to you with a business proposition. I'm not looking for an answer straight away, but would you be up for doing two or three cakes a week for me to sell slices of here? We can have a proper meeting about the finer details of money and all that stuff, if you want? You can pop down with your husband one evening and we can talk about it properly.'

'Oh, wow.' Catherine was stunned. This would guarantee an income each week and get her name out there. 'That sounds great. I'll definitely need to talk it over with my husband but will certainly call you if you give me your number.'

'I was hoping you'd say that.' She pulled a pen out of her pocket, along with a small notepad and wrote down her number. She tore off the piece of paper and handed it to Catherine. 'Here you go. We're free most evenings, so let me know when you're coming. Obviously your name will be on the cake menu board so people will know where they have come from. I won't steal your glory.'

'Fantastic, thank you. I'll speak to you soon.'

Anne left her at the table and after an hour the girls came in to say they were hungry.

'Your dad will be home soon, Bella, and he's bringing fish and chips with him for us to have for tea, but I think we can have a cheeky biscuit before we go.' She waved at Anne who was listening. 'Go tell Anne which one you want and we can eat them on the way home.'

The girls picked out a cookie each and they walked back to the house together. Although a deal hadn't been made with Anne yet, Catherine's head was already full of wonderful cake ideas. She couldn't wait to tell Adam but would save it for when the girls were in bed.

An hour later, Adam arrived home and the smell of fish and chips filled the house. Catherine could feel her tummy rumbling as she unpacked the food onto four plates. Adam snuck up behind her and kissed her on the cheek whilst sneakily pinching a chip from her plate.

'Oi! Cheeky git.' She laughed. 'Go and get the girls, will you?'

Adam went upstairs to bring the girls down for their tea. They ran down the stairs together and giggled as they took their seats at the table, clearly enjoying a private joke.

'Would you like any ketchup, Janey?'

'Yes, please,' she said politely, 'thank you.' Catherine put some on the side of her plate and then some onto Bella's plate too, knowing she would want some.

'Let me know if you'd like any more.'

They tucked into their freshly cooked hot fish and chips. The girls were quiet as they ate quickly, eager to go back upstairs. Once their plates were empty they asked if they could return to Bella's room.

'Yes but come back down soon and we can watch a film. Have

you seen *The Jungle Book*, Janey?' Janey shook her head. 'Well, before bed we can watch that, okay?'

'Yes, Mummy,' Bella said.

'We have some nice pudding too. We can eat it whilst we watch the film. Go on then, off you go.'

The girls ran back upstairs. They heard their footsteps as they went into Bella's room and closed the door.

'Do you think Charlotte will pop by tonight?' Adam asked.

'I'm not sure. Hopefully not. We don't want Janey telling her mum; she'll never let her come over again. She'll tell all the other parents too and then no one will come to Bella's birthday party.'

'Let's hope it's a peaceful night then.'

Later on, once the film had finished and they had eaten their warm chocolate brownies and ice cream, Catherine was expecting the girls to be tired; however, they looked as awake and excited as they had done at Dory's Corner. They were sent up to bed at nine o'clock but Catherine suspected they would be awake for a while. Catherine took this opportunity to tell Adam about Anne and the offer she had made.

'That sounds wonderful,' he said. 'Did you agree?'

'Not yet. I said I'd talk to you first. What do you think?'

'Well, if you get into a contract it'll guarantee an income. You'll become well known in the village and could probably up your prices for private customers. I think it's great. Definitely go for it. We can go see her next week. It might mean you won't have as much time for private customers, though. What do you think about that?'

'Well, I could always keep making cakes when family or friends ask for them. And if someone else calls up and I can't fit them in, I can always say no. Things like wedding cakes, though, are usually booked months in advance. So, I could easily plan that around baking cakes for the café. I might go for it. We could always try it out for a few months and see how it goes. I had loads of ideas on the way home.'

'Then you definitely should. Anything that makes you this happy and excited has to be done.'

As the evening wore on, Adam and Catherine decided it was time to go to bed. Adam had work in the morning so did not want to stay up much longer.

'I'll just check on the girls and tell them they need to go to sleep now,' Catherine said as they climbed the stairs together. She walked along to Bella's room and heard Janey talking about Charlotte. She listened at the door before going in.

'You said Charlotte would be here. Where is she?'

'She doesn't come all the time. I don't know where she is,' Bella whispered.

'Are you both in bed?' Catherine walked through the door. 'It's past eleven now, definitely time to go to sleep.'

Bella was in her own bed and Janey was in the blow-up bed on the floor next to her.

'But we're not tired, Mummy.'

'Well, don't make too much noise. Your dad has to be up for work in the morning. I'll leave your door slightly open and the landing light on, okay?' She thought this would make things easier for Janey in case she needed the toilet in the night. 'Goodnight, girls.'

'Goodnight,' they both said together.

She crossed back over the landing and into her bedroom to join Adam. He was sitting up in bed checking his alarm was set for the morning. He needed to be up at six o'clock.

'Do you think they're going to go to sleep?'

'Absolutely not.' Catherine got into bed. 'They're far too giddy. They were talking about Charlotte, though. Janey asked where she was. So Bella has definitely been mentioning her.'

'Well, there's no sign of her so fingers crossed it'll all be okay.'

They turned off their lamps and tried to go to sleep, listening to the background noise of the girls' chatter. They both took some comfort in the fact that this time it was actually the sound of their daughter and not Charlotte.

~

The scream startled them awake. Without thinking Catherine jumped out of bed, Adam right behind her, and ran straight to Bella's room. The landing light had been switched off and the bedroom door was shut. They tried to open it, but it was stuck. They pushed and pushed on the door handle but something was stopping it moving. They could hear Janey crying inside.

'Bella? Bella, can you open the door? What's going on?' Adam called. Catherine tried the light switch but it didn't work.

'It's Charlotte. She shut the door!' Bella shouted over Janey's cries.

'Are you both away from the door? Stand back, I'm going to break it open,' Adam called out loudly over Janey's cries.

In one push the door burst open and the landing light came back on at the same time. Both girls sat cuddled on the bed. Bella was wide-eyed but calm; Janey was very upset.

'What happened?' Catherine ran over to check they were okay.

'It was Charlotte. Janey was asleep. But Charlotte woke me up. She wanted me to go outside with her and to bring Janey. Then Janey woke up and saw her and screamed. Charlotte then disappeared but the door slammed shut.'

'Janey, are you okay? Don't pay any attention to Charlotte, she doesn't mean you any harm. Do you want me to call your mum and dad?'

Janey shook her head. Seeing Bella so calm helped to calm her down too. 'No, I think it just made me jump, that's all.'

'Are you sure? We can call them if you want?'

'No.' She wiped her face. 'I'm okay. I promise, I'm okay.'

Adam checked the time; it was three o'clock. 'What are the chances of them going back to sleep?' he asked Catherine.

'Girls, why don't the three of us grab some blankets and we can go downstairs and sleep on the couch?' She looked at Adam. 'I'll go down with them so they're not on their own and then you can have the last few hours of sleep.'

'Are you sure?'

'Yes, it's fine. You're at work in the morning, you need to sleep. We'll put a film on and I'm sure they'll drift off in no time.'

'All right. Take our duvet, it'll cover the couch. I'll borrow Bella's.'

The three of them headed downstairs and made a makeshift bed out of the couch. They all fit under the duvet and whilst watching *Finding Nemo* soon fell back to sleep. The rest of the night was quiet and uneventful. Charlotte had had her fun and had gone back to wherever she hid herself. Catherine knew she would need to tell Gillian what had happened. She just hoped it wouldn't have any consequences for any future visits from Janey.

CHAPTER 27

*C*atherine only briefly woke up as Adam left for work. She quickly fell back to sleep and didn't wake up again until half past eight. The girls were cuddled up together, still in a deep sleep. She carefully got up, trying not to wake them, and headed to the kitchen. Next to the kettle was a note from Adam:

Hope you got some sleep. See you tonight. Love you X

This made her smile. It reminded her of when they had first moved in together, and he would frequently leave her little notes if he was up early for work. One of those mornings had been an anniversary of theirs, and next to the note she'd found a pair of new earrings. He was always thoughtful and romantic.

Catherine switched on the kettle and went upstairs to fetch her mobile phone in case Gillian tried to call her. She sent a message to Adam to let him know that she was up and not too tired, and then made herself a coffee before sitting at the dining table in silence.

Twenty minutes later she heard the girls talking.

'Would you two like some breakfast?' Catherine asked as she popped her head around the door.

'Yes, please!' they replied.

'Are you both okay this morning? Janey? How are you feeling after last night?'

'I'm fine. It wasn't bad really. I don't know why I cried.'

'As long as you're sure you're okay. I'll talk to your mum when she comes.'

Catherine went back into the kitchen and made them all sausages, scrambled eggs and toast. She heard a message come through on her phone. It was Gillian:

Good morning. Hope you got enough sleep and weren't kept up too late! Will pick Janey up on our way home. Will be with you about 11.

Catherine replied:

That's fine, there's no rush. See you later.

She decided to leave out the events of the night until she saw Gillian in person.

Gillian knocked on the door just after eleven o'clock.

'Do you both want to come in?' Catherine asked, seeing that Steven was still in the car.

'Oh no, it's fine. Steven's wanting to get home to catch up on some work. Janey, say goodbye to Bella and thank you to Catherine for letting you stay.' Janey did as she was told and then made her way over to join her dad in the car. 'Thank you so much again. You really saved us. I would have hated to cancel. We owe you big time. Was she all right?'

'Well, actually...' Catherine told her what had happened, hoping Gillian wouldn't get too angry.

'Wow, really?' She looked up at the house. 'So, it really is... haunted?'

'Well, kinda. We're... looking into it. I hope you're not mad.'

'No, not at all. We can't help these things. There's been rumours about this house for as long as I can remember. I guess they're true. Janey wasn't harmed and you guys don't seem scared. Wow. I won't tell anyone, if that's what you're worrying about. Not everyone will take it the same way. My grandmother's house was haunted. I remember one time when I was little–' Steven beeped the car horn to hurry them up. 'Okay, okay, I'm coming!' she called to Steven. 'I should go. I'll see you on the school run tomorrow. Bye.'

Catherine and Bella waved them off as they drove away.

CHAPTER 28

June 1916

M ichael had finished his first week of work and he was loving it. It was easy and manageable and the children, who had been told to show him respect as a man who had been injured in the line of duty, admired him and were extremely polite. Charlotte enjoyed having him at the school. She always spoke to him when she saw him. Mary, however, kept away.

Mr Johnson made sure to tell him all he needed to know. At first, Michael followed him around, which was easy to do as Mr Johnson was very slow in his old age. He instructed Michael on the times to open and close the school and the order in which certain rooms were unlocked. There would be some cleaning to do but mainly maintenance. In the summer months when the school was closed Mr Johnson would repaint the doors and window frames to freshen them up in time for the new term. In December, he would order a Christmas tree and recruit a few pupils to help him with the decorations. There was a small garden area which he tended regularly and kept the flowers in bloom from spring until autumn.

Michael took in all the information he was given so that by the time Mr Johnson came to leave, he would have no problems taking over the role. For his lunches, he had collected sandwiches from Elizabeth each evening for the next day to begin with, but by the end of the second week he was just going round to her house to have his lunch there. On this Friday morning, however, they both skipped lunch. He was late back to the school. No one noticed, or at least, no one said anything to him about it. Maybe they took pity on him and presumed his leg was to blame.

Life had surely turned around for Michael. Once a recluse with no friends or confidence he was suddenly a very popular man in the village. Now he was working in the school, people knew his name and would be sure to say hello when they saw him in the market.

Things with Elizabeth had also changed. She was no longer pushing him away but had given in to her desires. Their affair was very well hidden. They had the perfect alibi. Henry had asked for Michael to be looked after and that is what the village would think was happening. They didn't know that he spent some nights in her bed. The children were too young to notice, but he was up to leave before they were out of bed anyway.

Deep down they both knew it had to end some time, but they never spoke about it. Henry would be home in just two months. Their affair had a deadline.

CHAPTER 29

*E*lizabeth quickly bundled up the coats that had been given to her by the church's charity to repair for the homeless. She had to return them to the vicar before the end of the day so set off from home in a hurry, almost dropping them on the path. It had taken her slightly longer than usual to get them mended as her days had been interrupted by Michael. She took Toby to spend the day with Henry's aunt Ruth while the girls were at school. She was confused by the reception she got from Ruth when she dropped off Toby. It was quite cold, not much conversation, but Elizabeth just put it down to Ruth's age. She was in her eighties. There was no other reason for it that Elizabeth could think of.

Elizabeth made her way from Ruth's house straight to the church. As she walked in through the main door she saw the vicar deep in conversation with Mrs Holmes; it looked like something serious. They both stopped talking immediately when they saw her walking towards them.

'Come and see me anytime, Alice. I'm sure it's nothing to worry about.'

'Right you are, Father.' Mrs Holmes turned to leave. She

walked past Elizabeth, nodding at her in acknowledgement but she did not stop to talk or ask about Henry as she normally did. Elizabeth began to suspect that the elderly village residents were having a very bad day indeed.

'Mrs Jones,' the vicar said, smiling, 'it is wonderful to see you. Can I offer you a cup of tea?'

'No thank you, Father, I can't stay.' Michael would be at her house soon for his lunch. 'I have finished the coats you sent to me. I'm sorry I took so long with them. I have just called in to drop them off.'

'Please, I must insist.' His tone had changed. 'Let's talk.'

'Okay.' This seemed serious, Elizabeth thought. She went to sit in one of the pews but he motioned for her to follow him. They walked into his office where they would not be disturbed.

'How is young Michael getting along? I hear he has settled in at his job at the school.'

'Yes.' She sat down whilst he poured freshly boiled water into a teapot. 'He is doing very well. He has certainly changed from the man he was when I first met him. He's just about to finish his third week at the school.'

'And you're back in contact with him now, then? You see him regularly? You stopped for a while, worried that people would get the wrong idea, didn't you?'

'Yes, he has become a close family friend I would say. He lives alone so I usually make his lunch for work to keep him going.'

'I see. And how is Henry? Do you hear from him much?'

'He usually writes every other day but sometimes his letters don't get delivered for a few weeks at a time.'

'And you write to him too? To keep his spirits up?'

'Yes, as often as I can.' She could not understand the reason for all these questions. He poured out the tea and some milk into two white cups. 'Postage isn't very cheap, though, so sometimes I wait until I have a few letters to send together.'

'I see.' He handed her one of the cups.

'I really can't stay for long, Father.'

'Elizabeth, some news has reached my ears. It is very serious and disturbing. I am hoping it is just rumour and not in fact truth.'

'Oh?' Elizabeth suddenly felt butterflies in her tummy. 'And, err... what are the rumours?'

'That your friendship with Michael is more than just helping him to get back onto his feet – excuse the poor choice of words there. It is believed that he occasionally spends the night. Is this true?'

'Well... sometimes. It is easier for him if he has been working late at the house. There is nothing improper about it.'

'So Henry is aware of this?'

'Well, to an extent, but I know he would not mind.'

'And what about your physical relationship with Michael? Would Henry not mind about that either?'

She didn't know what to say. 'Physical relationship?'

'Michael has been seen leaving your house at a very early hour, Elizabeth. Whilst I admit that hearing that troubled me deeply, I accepted there was nothing to read into it. However, apparently, on one of those mornings you were seen kissing in the doorway.' Elizabeth was stunned. 'I am hoping that you are going to tell me this is a lie and that I need to apologise for insulting you with this conversation.'

Tears quickly filled her eyes. Her lip quivered and her hands shook. *How could I have been so irresponsible?* she thought.

'Father, I... it's not... I mean, oh dear.' She burst into tears. The vicar allowed her time to compose herself.

'Elizabeth, I have known you and your family for a long time. I know that if Henry had not been sent away then this would never have happened. You have been left in a vulnerable position. Michael is just as much to blame here. I am not excusing your behaviour, but I am giving you a chance to end it. End the affair, end the rumours. These have reached Mrs Holmes, so God knows who else suspects.' Elizabeth nodded in agreement. Her hands were on the table and the vicar put his own over hers. 'Do the right thing. End it.'

～

'There you are. I was wondering what was taking you so long.' Michael had been sitting at the kitchen table waiting for Elizabeth. When he heard her come through the door, he got up to meet her and saw her red eyes and tear-stained cheeks. He immediately thought that Henry had been killed. 'What on earth has happened? Not Henry...'

'No, not Henry. You. Me. Us. We've been seen, Michael.'

'What? How?'

'At the door. People know you have been spending the night here and they saw us kiss when you left one morning. We have to end it, Michael. We can't carry on.'

'No.' He shook his head and walked into the living room. 'No, I won't accept this. I am not leaving you, Elizabeth. I love you.'

'You can't love me. I'm married.' She followed him into the room.

'I don't care. I love you. I am not going to lose you, not now.'

'Michael, don't make this any harder than it already is.' They were both crying now. 'I will lose my home and my children. Please don't make me choose between you and them.'

'Do you love Henry?'

'He's my husband!'

'That's not what I asked. Do you love Henry?'

'Of course I love Henry.'

'Do you love me?'

'Michael...'

'Do you love me?' he repeated, slowly. He walked up to her and held her face in his hands looking deep into her eyes. 'If you say you don't love me, then I will leave. But if you do love me, I will fight for you. I mean it. I will do everything and anything to make you mine. I'll ask you again, do you love me?'

'I... I can't answer.'

'Do you love me?' His lips edged closer to hers, until they were touching. It was a passionate kiss. Their tongues met. Neither of them had the power to pull away, but Elizabeth knew she had to. She had to take the vicar's advice.

'You need to go.' She could not look at him. She looked at the floor, avoiding his eyes. His hands slowly dropped from her face. 'You need to go back to work, and then you need to go home. To *your* home. We can never see each other again. I love my husband. When he comes home I will be honest with him and tell him what has happened. I will face the consequences. It is up to him what he wants to do with me.'

After a moment's silence to take in what Elizabeth was saying, Michael spoke, 'You're sure that is what you want? After everything? This is it?'

'Yes,' she said firmly. 'It's over.'

Michael stared at her for a while longer, hoping she would look up so he could see her eyes one more time, but she did not move. She stayed still, frozen. He slowly stepped back and then turned away. At the door, he paused, hoping she would change her mind and call him back, but there was no sound. He opened the door, stepped outside, and closed it behind him, not quite able to believe that it had all ended so quickly. As he walked down the path, he saw two women in a neighbouring garden talking intently whilst watching him, shaking their heads.

CHAPTER 30

*E*lizabeth sat in the living room. Toby was playing by her feet on the floor, but she was too distracted to notice him. Several days had gone by since she had last seen Michael and told him to leave. She had not heard from him since that day. She was heartbroken, but knew it was the right thing to do. She felt very lonely, more than she had when Henry had left. She could never admit it to Michael but she really was in love with him too. If she had been honest with him then he never would have left. She'd had to break his heart in order to end the affair, but it didn't mean she couldn't mourn that it was over. *It is for the best*, she told herself, *he's young and needs to find someone his own age who is not married. He will move on.*

She held in her hand a letter from Henry. It arrived two days ago, but she could not bring herself to open it. She had not written to him for a while. It was time to read it.

My dearest wife,

I can't believe the news I have just received. I will be leaving here on the 10th July. I will spend three weeks at the hospital again and then I will be on my way home to you for August. I cannot believe I have been away for four months. It feels like a lifetime.

I was sorry to hear of Michael's father. I hope he is coping well. I know you are there to support him, as you have been through it as well. Look after him. Do what is needed and tell him I will be home soon to do what I can for him.

Make sure to pass on the news to the children for me. I will write to them soon.

All my love,

your Henry.

Elizabeth felt so much guilt every time Henry mentioned Michael in his letters. Seeing his name written in Henry's handwriting made her feel sick. She was suddenly light-headed.

'Just wait there, Toby,' she said as she got up. 'I won't be long.'

She went up to the bathroom and was sick in the toilet. She couldn't think of any reason for being ill, unless it was stress or heartbreak. Or... *Surely not*, she thought. She stood in the bathroom for a moment going over dates in her head. When was her last period? It was some time before the first night she spent with Michael, possibly the beginning of April. If she was pregnant, there would be no way she could disguise it as Henry's. Everyone would know the truth. She had no idea what she was going to do. She heard the front door open and the girls return home from school.

'Mum?' Charlotte shouted. 'Mum, where are you?'

She wiped the tears from her eyes. 'I'm here. I'll be down in a minute.' She took a deep breath and then made her way downstairs to find the girls in the kitchen. Toby had also joined them. Mary picked him up.

'Are you hungry, Toby? Mum, I think he's hungry.'

'Well, why don't I make some sandwiches for us and you three can play in the garden?'

'It's too hot outside, Mum. It's been scorching all day. It's nice and cool in here.' Mary looked at the basket of clothes by the back door. Elizabeth had washed them all but not taken them outside. 'Did you forget to hang those out?'

'Oh, damn. Yes, I did forget. I've not been well today, Mary. They'll need washing again.'

'Charlotte and I can wash them. They'll be dry by tonight if we put them out straight away.'

'You can do them tomorrow. It's Saturday so you won't have to rush. Don't worry about it.' She smiled at Mary; she didn't know what she would do without her. 'Come on, sit down and I'll make us all some sandwiches. Tell me about your day.'

'Michael hasn't been at school for days,' Charlotte said.

'Where has he been?' She tried to sound casual.

'Mr Johnson has had to do everything on his own again. No one knows where he is. Have you seen him?' Mary asked.

'No, I haven't.' It was the truth. 'I've not seen him for a few days. Maybe he's poorly.'

'Shall we go and see him?' Charlotte jumped off her chair.

'No,' Elizabeth said quickly. Charlotte sat back down. 'No, there's no need. He's a grown man; he's back on his feet. Your dad wanted us to support him and we did. He needs to look after himself now.'

The girls were quiet at the table. They didn't question her any further. Elizabeth prepared some sandwiches for the children. She would not be eating as she was still feeling sick. She wasn't going to tell Michael about it, but hearing that he had gone missing felt the need to check that he was okay. She would have to go to his house tomorrow.

'Your dad has sent a letter with some good news. He will be home at the start of August. That's just over a month away. Isn't that exciting?' The girls beamed. 'Why don't we all write him a letter? I think he'll really like that. Once we've eaten, I'll get us some paper and we can get on with it. I can send them to be posted tomorrow.'

My dearest Henry,

I have just received your letter. I am so glad you will be leaving that place soon and spending your final weeks there in the hospital. At least I know you will be out of danger.

Michael is doing very well. Mr Stubbs has given him the job of caretaker of the school. Mr Johnson will be retiring in the summer. Now he has this job I don't see him as often anymore. He is back on his feet and making a life for himself.

I am so looking forward to your return. I have been very lonely.

Your one and only,

Elizabeth.

CHAPTER 31

Once the girls had left for school in the morning and Toby had been taken to Aunty Ruth's, Elizabeth picked up all their letters and set off for the post office. She was dreading bumping into Mrs Holmes but luckily on this particular morning she was not sitting in her garden. It was early so there were not many people in the village yet. Elizabeth was glad; she was not sure how far the gossip about her and Michael had spread.

She reached Michael's cottage and knocked on the door. The door and windows had finally been cleaned and the outside tidied up. It was starting to look lovely and cosy. She knocked again and when there was no answer wondered if he had gone back to the school today. She began to walk away when the door opened and there Michael stood. He was unshaven and his hair was a mess.

'What are you doing here?' he asked.

'I was just checking you were okay. Charlotte said you hadn't been at school.' She smiled at him, but he did not smile back. He only stared at her. 'So, are you?'

'I'm fine.'

'Why haven't you been going to the school?'

'You shouldn't have come here. You told me to stay away and I did. Why would you come here?'

Elizabeth looked around to check no one could hear the conversation. 'Why don't we talk inside, Michael?'

He looked at her and thought about it for a moment before moving to one side to let her walk past him. She stepped inside and saw that he had definitely been keeping himself busy. She couldn't believe how much the inside had changed. The hard wood floors had been scrubbed and cleaned, the curtains had been washed, the shelves dusted, and the kitchen looked almost new.

'Well, this all looks amazing. You've done really well here, Michael.' She turned around to smile at him. He was standing sheepishly by the door. 'Why haven't you been at the school, Michael? It's a good job for you and an opportunity you shouldn't waste.'

'I've spoken to Stubbs. He has allowed me time off to sort some things out. He said I can start properly in September. I've been shown what to do and there isn't long left before the summer break. He came around to see me and saw what the house was like, so said to take all the time I need and then be back in the new school year.'

'Oh, well that's good then. I was worried that–'

'Worried about what?' he interrupted her. 'Why are you worried? You made yourself perfectly clear.'

'Michael, I–'

'No, I don't want to hear it. You didn't want me. You broke my heart. You have no right to come around here and tell me you were worried about me.'

'Please, don't be like that. Henry will be home soon; he will want to see you.'

'I don't want to see Henry. Why would I want to see him?

You've chosen to be with him and I'm sure you two will live happily ever after, whether you tell him or not.'

'I have to tell him…' she began to say. 'I thought about not telling him but something has happened, and now I can't avoid telling it.'

'What's happened?' he asked. She looked at the floor to avoid his eyes. 'Well? What is it?'

She looked up at him. 'I'm pregnant, Michael.'

He stepped back, his mouth opened to speak but words failed him. He walked into the kitchen and sat down at the table. Elizabeth didn't know whether to follow him or not but decided to give him a few minutes to himself. She looked around the living room at the pictures on the wall. There was only one photo amongst them. It was of a young woman. She was pretty. Elizabeth assumed she was Michael's mother.

Five minutes later Michael walked back into the room.

'Are you sure? I mean, you're definitely pregnant?'

'Yes, Michael. I've been ill and…' She wasn't sure how much detail he would want. It didn't matter with Henry; he was a doctor as well as her husband and could listen to her talk about periods and cycles. 'I'm definitely pregnant.'

'And, err, it's not Henry's?'

'No, when I last saw him in February we weren't… intimate. It can only be yours.'

'Elizabeth, I…' He stepped towards her and held her hands. 'I can't believe it. This is wonderful.'

'Wonderful? How on earth is this wonderful?' She pulled away from him and stepped back. 'This is going to kill Henry. The first time he sees me I'm going to be showing. People around here will all know the truth before he even gets home. This is far from wonderful.' She turned around putting her back to him.

'It is wonderful. I'm going to be a dad. And you will be the mum. Elizabeth–' He walked up behind her and held her shoulders. '–I love you. We need to be together. This is our chance. Let's go, now.'

'Go?' She turned around to face him. 'What on earth are you talking about?'

'Let's leave now. Just us. We can go somewhere no one knows us. No one has to know the truth.'

'I'm not leaving my family.'

'And what are you going to do when Henry gets home, hmm? He'll kick you out. He won't forgive you for this. Like you said, you will lose your home and your children. But if we leave now, with the children, you won't have anything to worry about.'

'I have to go, you're being absurd.'

'No.' He blocked her way of the door. 'We're talking about this. I know you love me. I could tell last time I saw you, when you were telling me to leave and you couldn't look me in the eye. You knew that if you did, you would change your mind. You're doing this because you think it's the right thing to do, and yes it probably is, but what do *you* want?'

'Michael, I have to go. I came around to check on you. Charlotte was worried. I can tell her now that you're fine, but I need to leave.'

'No.' He held her arms. 'I can't let you leave; I can't lose you. I don't want to lose you. I want to be with you.'

'Well we can't!' she cried. 'We can't, Michael.' She looked into his eyes. 'I have to go.'

They stared at each other for a moment. Michael couldn't resist, and he leaned in to kiss her. As he had with their first kiss, he expected her to push him away, but she didn't. Elizabeth let him kiss her.

'Oh, Michael. I'm in such a mess. I love you, but I don't know what to do.'

'You do love me?'

'Yes, of course I do. I don't want to lose you either.'

'Then we have to leave.'

'No, we're not leaving. We're not going anywhere. I love you, Michael, I do, but this does have to end. That was a goodbye kiss. And I will have to go now. If anyone saw me come in here they will think we're doing something.'

'Can I come by tonight? After the children are asleep? I'll be gone before the sun comes up. No one has to see.'

'No, you can't. You have to let me go.'

'Elizabeth...'

'I have to go.'

'Please.'

'No! Now let me past. I have to go home.'

Michael stood to one side. Elizabeth opened the door and walked away. Michael watched her move off down the lane and out of sight. Before he stepped back inside he saw Mrs Holmes across the street. She was shaking her head at him.

'Disgustin', that's what you are. You should be ashamed!' she shouted.

'I don't know what you're talking about, Mrs Holmes.'

'Well, you soon will. I've a right to write to 'enry an' tell 'im myself.'

'It's none of your business, Mrs Holmes.'

'An' pregnant as well? I can tell. Looks exactly the same as she did with the others. She won't hide that for long.'

She walked away. Michael couldn't believe that she could already know about the baby. Would she really write to Henry? He'd have to warn Elizabeth. He decided to go see her later and convince her to leave. They would have to go that night.

CHAPTER 32

*M*ichael knew the children would be in bed and asleep by the time he was ready to set off to convince Elizabeth that they had to leave with him. Mrs Holmes knew about the baby and seemed determined to write to Henry to tell him what had been going on. Even if Henry forgave her, Elizabeth would never be treated the same again by her neighbours or anyone who knew her and in a village as small as this one everyone knew each other. No matter what happened, Michael was determined not to lose her. This was his last chance.

He packed a modest-sized bag; he did not have many belongings. Then he picked up the small amount of money he had saved and said goodbye to his father's house. He would not be returning.

He'd waited until it was fully dark outside, as he didn't want anyone to see him leave with Elizabeth and the children or where they were going. He walked down the small snickets and climbed over walls to stay off the road and out of sight. It didn't take him long to reach Elizabeth's house, where he could see lit candles through the living room window. The fire wasn't glowing but it had been a very warm evening. On his walk to the house he wondered how to break the news to Elizabeth about Mrs Holmes. He didn't want to scare her, but maybe that would be the only way to finally convince her to leave with him. It was the truth after all.

Michael walked down the garden path and knocked lightly on the door. When there was no answer he gently called out Elizabeth's name. The door opened.

'Michael, do you know what time it is?' She was dressed only in her nightgown. 'What on earth are you doing here? You can't be here now. If anyone saw you...'

'Please, you need to hear this.' He walked past her, and she quickly closed the door behind him. 'There's something you need to know.'

'You can't stay here, Michael. The children...'

'They're asleep. Please listen to me.'

'I can't leave with you. I won't leave. This is my home,' she said firmly.

'Mrs Holmes knows.'

'I know she knows. She told the vicar about us.'

'No, I saw her earlier after you left. She knows you're pregnant. I don't know how she knows but she does. And she intends to write to Henry to tell him.'

Elizabeth went pale. She walked into the living room. 'She... she knows? Why is she going to write to him? It's none of her business. Why would she do that? Are you sure?' She was now pacing around the room in a panic. 'What am I going to do? He can't hear it from her. It'll destroy him enough without hearing it from someone else first. What can I do?'

'You can leave with me. It's the only option. Get some things, get the children, and let's go. If she tells the rest of the village it will be hell for you and the children. You're carrying my baby and I don't want either of you to suffer.'

'We can't leave, Michael. Where on earth would we go?'

'Scotland. I have family up there. We could say you're a

widow and we've since married. No one up there would question it.'

'The girls, though, they would know the truth. Mary would never accept it.'

'We'll have to tell them that Henry died,' Michael said as Elizabeth scoffed at the idea. 'That's the only way around it. They'd never see him again anyway. It's the only way to make it work.'

Elizabeth looked at Michael and for the first time he felt sure that she would agree to his plan.

'There must be something else we can do, anything.'

'Like what? Henry receives a letter from Mrs Holmes, laughs it off and writes back to you that the three of us will all live happily ever after! It won't happen. You know it's going to end badly whatever he decides. He'll stop us seeing each other. I can't be apart from you. And will he let you keep the baby? This way–' He held her hands. '–I can keep you safe. Both of you.'

Elizabeth thought about this for a moment. She loved Henry, she did; they had been married a long time and had three beautiful children. It would be incredibly selfish to leave and most of all to lie about his death to the children, but she couldn't think of another way around it. He might decide to divorce her which would leave her without a home or her children. She could not imagine leaving them. She also could not guarantee the safety of her unborn child. The price of Henry's forgiveness might be to give up the baby and she could not do that either. She was in love with Michael, she couldn't deny that, and right now he wanted her, the baby and the children.

'I'm going to hell,' she said.

'Is that a yes?' he asked. 'Will you come with me?'

'Yes, I'll come.'

Michael breathed a huge sigh of relief. Tears of happiness filled his eyes. He opened his arms and Elizabeth fell into them. They held each other closely.

'When do we go?' she asked.

'Now.'

'No, not now. We have no money to go anywhere and it's dark. We'll go first thing in the morning.'

'Okay.' He kissed her head. 'Go upstairs and pack some things.' She headed out the room and towards the stairs. 'I'll make us a drink. Elizabeth–' She turned around. '–are you really coming with me? Do you mean it?'

'Yes, I do.' She smiled, not quite believing what she was saying. 'I love you, Michael.'

'I love you too.'

She turned and hurried up the stairs to her bedroom. Michael walked into the kitchen to make them both a drink. In his entire life he had never felt so happy. They were finally leaving together. This was it.

CHAPTER 33

June 2016

'What if it rains tomorrow?' Bella asked as she looked out the kitchen window. The sky was blue and it had been a glorious day.

'It won't rain tomorrow. The weatherman says so,' Catherine said as she loaded the dishwasher. They had just finished their tea and were planning on a quiet evening, but Bella was too excited about her birthday party tomorrow. 'Anyway, Aunty Emma promised that she would bring the sun with her from London. She'll be here nice and early to help us set up.'

'But what if no one comes?'

'All your classmates are coming; it will be fine. Relax.'

'Can I see the cake?'

'No, that's a surprise for tomorrow.'

'Oh, please, Mummy!'

'Definitely not! Go watch telly. Your dad will be watching footy but tell him to stick a film on for us instead.'

'Okay.' Bella jumped down off the dining chair and headed out of the kitchen. As she walked past the front door there was a quick and excitable knock. 'Mummy, shall I open it?'

'I'm coming, hang on.' Catherine looked at her watch and wondered who could be coming around on a Friday evening. She opened the door. 'Oh my God, Emma! What are you doing here already?'

Emma laughed as she walked in with her bags. She was wearing a short, dark denim skirt, a white short-sleeved shirt and tan sandals. Emma and Catherine hugged as Adam came to join them.

'Hey, sis! And Bella and Adam.' She hugged them all one at a time. 'I managed to get today off work so thought I'd come up early. And I'm yours for a week if you'll have me? They don't need me at work next week.'

'Course we'll have you.' Emma had originally planned to come just for the Saturday night but this would be a lot better. 'You don't even need to ask. I can't believe you've got a week off work. How'd you manage that?' They all walked into the kitchen and Emma placed her bags on the table.

'Well, we did this pitch for Virgin and it was down to us and this other agency. We were sure that we had it in the bag, but yesterday they just blew us off and went with the other guys. My boss was so pissed off, especially with all the work we'd put into it, so he's given our team a break and told us to take the week off. Such a waste of all that effort.'

'Aw, I'm sorry it didn't work out.'

'Well, balls to them, that's what I say. It just happened to fall on my weekend off so I can stay up here with you a little longer. I'm sure tomorrow is somebody's birthday but I can't remember whose.' She looked from Catherine to Adam while Bella giggled. 'Adam, is it your birthday?'

'Nope, not mine.'

'Oh dear. Cat, is it yours?'

'Nope, not mine either.'

'Hmm, that's very strange.' She reached into one of her bags and pulled out several wrapped presents. Bella was still giggling. 'Well, I don't know who to give these to then.'

'It's me, Aunty Emma. It's my birthday. I'm six tomorrow.' She jumped up and down.

'Six? Are you sure?'

'Yes! Look at the calendar.' She pointed at the fridge. 'Look, it says, "Saturday 11 June, Bella's birthday and party"!'

'Oh, so it is! Well, I will hold on to these until tomorrow, except this one.' She pulled out a small package. 'You'll need to open this one tonight if we're gonna be roomies for the next week.'

Bella thanked her and sat down at the table to open it. She pulled off the shiny pink paper to reveal a pink nightie with a white unicorn head on the front. As she was doing that, Emma reached into her other bag and pulled out an identical nightie in an adult size.

'We can be twins whilst I'm here.' She held it up so Bella could see.

'Wow, I love it! Thank you! Can we put them on now?'

'Maybe in a little while before we go to bed. I want a cuppa first.'

'I'll put the kettle on,' Adam volunteered. 'Bella, why don't you go get yourself ready for bed and I'll make you some chocolate milk for when you come back down.'

Bella ran upstairs.

'So, what's been happening since my last visit?' Emma asked when she knew Bella was out of earshot.

Catherine and Adam filled her in on everything that had happened in the house, finishing with the story of the night Elizabeth had almost suffocated Catherine.

'And you're still living here? Most people would have moved

out!' Emma's eyes were wide and she was no longer smiling. 'Cat, that is crazy. Why are you still here?'

'I don't think they're trying to hurt us. They're trying to tell us something. They want our help.'

'And if they don't get it they kill you, is that it?'

'No, we're fine, we're working it out.'

'That's the only physical contact they've made with us,' Adam said. 'It's not something you can call the police in for, so, other than calling in the Ghostbusters, we have to sort it out ourselves. It's not like we have the money to just move out. We put it all into buying this place.'

'I feel like, if we can find out what they want it will all come to an end. They'll be at peace.'

'But they just disappear as soon as they talk to you?'

'Pretty much.'

Emma took in what they had told her. She wasn't scared but she felt a bit uneasy.

'How is Bella coping with it all?'

'She doesn't know anything other than what she has seen herself,' Catherine said. 'It's nothing to be scared of, but we don't want to freak her out.'

'Talk of the devil,' Adam said as they heard Bella running down the stairs and into the kitchen to show off her new nightie.

'Whit-woo!' Emma said. 'You look fabulous, darling.' Bella beamed at being complimented by her trendy London aunty. 'So, tell me again, how old will you be tomorrow?'

'I'll be six.'

'Wow! That old? What time are your friends coming?'

Emma and Bella got into a conversation about the party. Adam went upstairs to set up the blow-up bed in Bella's room and Catherine made them all a drink. She made sure that all the food was ready for the next day and had one final check of the cake. It had been left in her room at the back of the kitchen with the door firmly shut. Bella was instructed not to take a sneaky peek.

CHAPTER 34

*E*mma was jolted awake in the morning as Bella jumped down from her bed and onto the blow-up bed where Emma had been sleeping.

'Good morning, you,' Emma said, stretching. 'What time is it?'

'It's half seven. I couldn't sleep any more. Charlotte kept tapping my head.'

'Charlotte?' she asked, sitting up in bed. 'Is she here now?' She looked around the room, no longer tired.

'No, she went when I told her I was awake. Didn't you see her?'

'No, I must have just missed her.'

'Are you going to make pancakes again like last time?'

'We'll have to ask your mum. She might have something else planned for breakfast. Go see if she's awake and I'll just nip to the bathroom.'

Bella jumped off the bed and ran out the room and into her parents' bedroom. Emma heard her almost crash through the door and jump on their bed, evidently straight onto Adam judging by the noise that came out of him. Emma laughed and got out of bed. She put a cardigan over her nightie and made her way to the bathroom with her toiletries bag. When she finished in the bathroom, she opened the door and was startled by Bella who was standing outside waiting for her.

'Mummy says we can have pancakes!'

'Ooh, good! Come on then, let's get them started.'

The morning went by very quickly. Pancakes were made and eaten, Bella opened her cards and presents, everyone had a shower and changed into their shorts and T-shirts. Bella had a special party dress for the occasion. The sky was a clear blue again and the weather promised to be barbeque friendly. Adam made sure the barbeque was set up and ready for their guests. Catherine loaded the table with food, having decided that it was too hot to leave it all outside. In no time at all, Bella's friends started to arrive with their enthusiastic mothers and not-so-excited fathers – who soon cheered up when the beer was brought out of the fridge.

Adam's parents arrived and showered Bella with gifts and hugs. They were the only other family to come to the party. Catherine's parents were somewhere in the south of France but had made sure to send a card with a cheque.

Games were played, food was eaten and more presents were unwrapped. Bella had never looked so happy as when her main present was unveiled in the garden: a play set with two swings, slide and seesaw. The children took turns to play.

Catherine was delighted with how the day went. Once everyone had gone, including Adam's parents, she, Adam and Emma sat in what was left of the evening sun with a beer each whilst Bella played on the swings.

'Well,' Emma started, 'I can honestly say that was the best party I've been to all year. Fact.'

'It was good, wasn't it!' Catherine agreed. 'I'm so glad

everyone came but I am glad they've gone too. I'm knackered. I need to chill now.'

'You deserve to chill, baby,' Adam said, kissing her hand. 'You did amazing today.'

'Not everyone has left, though,' Emma said. 'Who's that in your bedroom? Cheeky sods having a snoop around.'

Adam and Catherine looked up at their bedroom window just as Emma suddenly realised who it was. Elizabeth was standing in the same place she had been before. Her eyes were wide and sad, her hand on the glass.

'Is that her?' Emma asked. 'Is that Elizabeth? What is she looking at?'

'She's looking behind us, near Bella.'

'I'm going up.' Emma put her drink down.

'Wait!' Catherine tried to stop her.

'No, you said yourself you want to find out what they want. Now is our chance.'

'Too late,' Adam said, 'she's gone.'

'Dammit.' Emma sat back down and picked up her drink.

They were soon relaxed again and sat out together until the sun was lost behind the house, but Emma could not take her eyes from that window.

CHAPTER 35

'Where are you going for a walk?' Adam asked as he drank his coffee in the kitchen the next morning. He would be setting off for work soon and would not be back until late that night.

'Not sure, it's just for a stroll to make most of this weather before we get our usual summer of rain.' Catherine handed him his bag, which she had filled up with leftovers from the barbeque and a large slice of cake. There was a lot of cake left, and it was now sitting on the kitchen table ready to be cut into small pieces for Bella to hand out at school the next day.

'Thank you.' He kissed her and put his empty cup in the sink. Bella and Emma were in the living room in their matching nighties. He went to say goodbye. 'I'll see you two lazy monkeys tomorrow.'

'Bye!' they said together as he walked out the door and to the car.

'Right then, I'll go get dressed.' Emma stood up. 'Then we can go out. It looks like another day for shorts,' she said as she glanced out the window.

'Come on, Bella,' Catherine said, 'we'll need to put some sun cream on before you get dressed.'

Eventually, just after eleven o'clock, they were ready and headed out together. They walked through the busy market, filled with locals buying their freshly baked bread and recently chopped meat and tourists buying their themed tea towels and scented soaps, and wandered away from the noise and down a peaceful road.

'That's the old post office there,' Catherine pointed out. It was now just a Co-op but the words 'Post Office' were still etched into the stonework above the door although the year had eroded too much to be very clear.

'Must have been a bloody big post office.'

'No, I think that half of it was a cottage. You can see where there was a door at one point. You can tell where it's been filled in.'

'What a shame, looks like it was a beautiful little home at one point.'

They went inside to buy a cool drink each and carried on walking until they had managed a circle of the village and were almost back at the house. They were warm from the heat of the afternoon sun. When the house was in sight, Bella ran ahead to beat them to the door.

'Did you see Elizabeth when you went to bed last night?' Emma asked when Bella was a safe enough distance away not to hear her.

'No,' Catherine kept her voice low, 'it was a really peaceful night if I'm honest. No sound from anywhere apart from the owl that lives somewhere in the garden.' They walked down the garden path and caught up with Bella who was waiting by the door. 'How about we have some leftovers for a light lunch and then order in a pizza for tea?'

'Yeah!' Bella shouted.

'Sounds good to me,' Emma agreed.

'Okay.' Catherine unlocked the door. 'And we can watch a movie too. We can't have a late night though, Bella. You have school in the morning.'

'Yes, Mummy.' Bella ran in through the open door and immediately saw Barney. He had been placed in a sitting position on the top step of the stairs looking down on them all as they walked in.

'Did you leave him there, Bella?' Catherine asked.

'No, he was on the couch.'

Emma and Catherine exchanged looks while Bella ran up to retrieve him. Emma nodded, as she had seen Barney on the couch too just before they had set off.

'All right then, to the kitchen,' Catherine said. 'What would we all like to eat?'

The large pepperoni pizza was delivered at exactly seven o'clock. Catherine put it on the coffee table in the living room so they could all help themselves. Emma brought in a jug of pineapple juice with ice and three glasses. Bella picked a film and they all got comfy on the couch together.

'Right, are we ready, folks?' Catherine had the remote in her hand about to press play when there was a knock on the door. 'Dammit. Hang on, guys.' She stood and looked out the window but there was no one there. 'Weird, I can't see anyone.' She went to the door and opened it just in case someone was standing out of view of the living room window.

'Is anyone there?' Emma called from the couch.

'No, no one.' Catherine shut the door and sat back down with the others. 'Right, let's try again shall we?'

Footsteps thumped up the stairs. They all listened as the steps made their way slowly along the landing above their heads and stopped when they sounded like they were outside Bella's room.

'Who the chuff is that?' Emma asked.

'I don't know. Let's just get this film on and eat up before the pizza gets too cold.'

Twenty minutes into the film the noise started again. The footsteps seemed to run up and down the landing four times before stopping at the top of the stairs. Emma panicked and looked towards her sister, but she shook her head at her and nodded down at Bella between them who was happily watching the film. Catherine did not want to worry Bella who was nicely distracted.

Bang. All three of them jumped. Bang.

'What is it doing?' Emma sat up.

'It sounds like it's opening and shutting our bedroom doors.' Catherine placed a comforting hand on her daughter's leg.

Bang. Bang. Bang. The footsteps ran across the landing to each door. Bang. Bang. Bang. Then they ran down the stairs, crashing on every step as though a bowling ball had been dropped from the top. Bella was no longer watching the film. She stood up and clung on to her mum as the footsteps hit the bottom and seemed to run into the kitchen, eventually ending with a loud crash which made them all jump and Bella cry out. Silence.

'Is… is it done?' Emma asked.

'I don't know.' Catherine knew she had to go and see what the loud crash had been, but fear was keeping her legs from moving.

'Come on,' Emma said, reading her sister's expression. 'Let's all go together.'

They all stood up and held hands and, with Catherine leading, slowly walked to the living room door. Catherine stepped out first with Bella in the middle followed by Emma. Up the stairs there was nothing to be seen. They carried on walking into the kitchen to find out what had crashed to the floor. There was a tray with some plates and cutlery, Bella's school lunch box and the rest of her birthday cake. Each tier had fallen apart and was ruined.

'My cake!' she cried.

'It's okay, don't worry.' Emma hugged her whilst looking at her sister.

'We were supposed to cut it up,' Bella cried, 'and take it to school.'

'They'll understand. We'll say it was an accident.'

'Why did they do it?' she asked her mum.

'I don't know, darling. I honestly have no idea.'

Once Bella had settled down and the kitchen had been cleaned up they made their way back to the living room. They had a slice of cold pizza each and tried to laugh about what had happened to make Bella feel better about it.

'Clearly they're not a fan of your baking,' Emma joked.

'That was really funny, wasn't it, Bella? They've never done that before. Was it Charlotte? You'll have to tell her she upset you when she ruined your cake.'

'I will. I saw her this morning but she ran away from me. She looked angry.'

'Why would she be angry?'

'I don't know.'

They resumed the film and were able to watch it until the end with only one interruption when Adam telephoned to say he would be sleeping over at the station. He had had a busy night and was too tired for the long drive home. Had Catherine been alone with Bella he would have come back, but he knew she would be all right with Emma there and he'd be home first thing in the morning after a rest. Catherine opted not to tell him about what had happened as it would worry him. She would wait until she saw him in the morning.

The film finished just after nine o'clock. 'Well, madam, it is way past your bedtime now. Shall we take you up?'

'No, Mummy, I can go.'

'Are you sure?' Catherine was worried in case Charlotte was still around and 'angry', as Bella had said. 'I can come up with you if you want?'

'No, I'm fine.' She hopped off the couch.

'All right. Make sure you brush your teeth though, okay?' She opened her arms and Bella gave her a hug and a kiss goodnight before walking out and up the stairs.

'That is one brave child,' Emma said. 'There's no way I'm going up there alone. Not even to pee.'

'You big wuss. She's six and she isn't fazed by any of this. It's just us oldies that have seen too many horror films. I'd rather she was brave about it all. If I was alone tonight without both of you I would have been camping in the garden until Adam got home.'

'Ha-ha. Any more of this angry ghost and I'll be out there myself. I'll go put the kettle on. Shall I warm the rest of that up?' she asked, pointing at the pizza.

'Nah, not for me. I like it cold.'

Emma headed into the kitchen to make them both a drink and Catherine stood at the bottom of the stairs listening out for Bella to make sure she was okay. She heard her in the bathroom brushing her teeth and then watched her as she walked back down the landing to her bedroom. Catherine left the landing light on for her and joined Emma in the kitchen.

'Did you see Charlotte this morning, then?' she asked Emma.

'No, I've not seen her at all.' She poured the milk into the cups and stirred it into the coffee. They heard a bang above their heads. 'Is that Bella?'

'No, that was from the spare room above us. I saw Bella walk into her room.' It sounded again.

'Shall we go get Bella?'

'No, I don't want to scare her. It's not in her room. She'll be asleep in no time. Let's just listen and see what it does. We hear this quite a lot and it never comes to anything.'

They stood in the kitchen, not daring to move or make a

sound. All they could hear was gentle tapping in the room above and the whirring sound of the fridge. The rest of the house was silent. Eventually the noise above faded out.

'Okay, we're all good.' Emma picked up her cup of coffee.

The scream was deafening, high-pitched, and close to them. It was not from upstairs but from the living room. Emma dropped her cup on the floor and hot coffee splashed their legs, but they barely noticed. Instinctively they both clung to each other and looked towards the kitchen door. The scream stopped after a few seconds, but they could hear someone moving about in the living room. A child was crying.

Emma reached into her pocket and pulled out her phone, swiping to open the camera and set the video to record.

'What are you doing?' Catherine asked.

'We need to film whatever it is. Come on.' She grabbed Catherine's hand.

'Are you mad? This isn't *Most Haunted*.'

'If something or someone is in there, we need to talk to them. You need answers or you can't help them. Come on.' Emma pulled her sister forward and she reluctantly followed her. They walked across the hallway and stopped at the door. They looked in, holding the camera out in front, and tried to see what had made the noise.

There was nothing there. The room was empty.

'It was definitely coming from in here,' Emma said, stepping into the room with the camera, panning it around to try to catch something. She pointed it at her sister in the doorway who hated being filmed. 'Smile, you're on Emma's camera, coming soon to a haunted house near you.' She laughed. 'Cat! Behind you!' She quickly zoomed in on the girl standing by the stairs. Catherine looked back and saw her and jumped into the living room in a panic. The girl stared at them both. Their voices froze, as did their bodies, at the reality of what they were seeing.

Her eyes were wide. She stood directly under the light which shone on her fair, curly hair. Her dress was blue with white pin stripes and a lace collar. She lifted her hand and pointed at Emma before looking up the stairs and running quickly to the top.

'Shit, the camera.' Emma realised she'd lowered the camera in her alarm and had been filming their feet. She rushed after the little girl and pointed the camera up the stairs, only just catching her as she ran out of sight. They heard Bella's door slam shut.

'Bella!' Catherine shouted, sprinting up the stairs. No matter how scary the situation was, her instinct was to protect her daughter, and she suddenly felt no anxiety in facing her fears. Emma followed, still with the camera in hand. 'Bella!' They reached her door. Catherine tried the handle but it was jammed shut. 'Bella! Are you awake?' She banged on the door.

'Mummy?' Bella's voice called out. 'Why is the door shut?'

'I don't know, baby, but I can't open it. Can you see anything blocking it?' Catherine was trying her best to sound calm. 'Can you try to open it?'

She heard Bella pulling at the handle on the other side of the door. 'It won't open, Mummy.'

'Okay, are you all right? Is Charlotte in there with you?'

There was a pause before Bella answered. 'Yes, she's on my bed now. She's laughing.'

'Tell her it's too late to play games now. Can you tell her? We need to go to bed.'

'She's gone. She's just disappeared.'

Catherine tried the door again and it opened. She pulled Bella into her arms and knelt down on the floor to hug her.

'Are you okay? Did she do anything?'

'I'm fine. I was asleep when I heard you.'

'Catherine...' Emma said, softly.

'Why are you crying, Mummy?'

'I just panicked when I couldn't open the door, that's all. I came to check if you were okay.'

'Catherine!' Emma nudged her sister with her leg.

'What?' Catherine looked up and suddenly saw why Emma was trying to get her attention. Her bedroom door was wide open and by the bed stood Elizabeth. Emma pointed the camera at her but it was too dark to pick anything up.

'Who's that?' Bella asked, quietly.

'That's Elizabeth,' Catherine whispered. 'That's Charlotte's mother.'

Elizabeth was not looking at them. She was looking at the floor by the bedside table. They couldn't see her face. Turning slowly, still not looking at them, she walked around the bed and to the window, her long skirt flowing as she passed the door. She stopped once she reached the window and looked out into the garden. The house was silent. All Catherine could hear was the sound of her own heart as it beat strongly against her chest. Once again, they were all frozen, too scared to move.

Suddenly, the bedroom door slammed shut, as though it had been thrown by a strong force. Bella's door did the same. They all screamed and held on to each other not knowing where to turn.

'Downstairs!' Emma shouted, and together they ran down into the living room.

CHAPTER 36

*I*t was six o'clock in the morning when Adam arrived home. He had managed to get some sleep at the station but decided to come back for a shower and a change of clothes before returning to work in the afternoon. Also, had he stayed there until his next shift he would not have seen Catherine or Bella for a couple of days.

The sun was already up and he could feel its slight heat touching his face as he walked down the garden path. He unlocked the door and walked in, leaving his shoes at the bottom of the stairs. He had planned on going straight up to let Catherine know he was home but something caught his eye. He looked into the living room and saw Emma curled up asleep in the armchair. When he walked in he then spotted Catherine on the couch holding Bella close under a blanket.

'Catherine,' he whispered as she stirred and opened her eyes. Very gently she got up, leaving Bella under the blanket, and followed him into the kitchen. 'Late night was it?' he said, smiling.

'You could say that.' She rubbed her eyes.

They walked into the kitchen and Adam saw the broken cup and coffee on the floor.

'What happened here?'

Catherine filled him in on everything, from the noises upstairs to the crash which had resulted in Emma dropping her coffee.

'Are you kidding?'

'Take a look for yourself.' She pointed at the bin.

Adam lifted the lid and there it was, Bella's cake, as well as two broken plates. He was speechless.

'And you say Emma was filming it?'

'She had her camera on, but we've not checked it yet to see what she caught. We'll have a look at it once Bella has gone to school.'

Emma joined them in the kitchen.

'Have you told him?' She yawned.

'Yes, she has. Can I see your phone?'

Emma unlocked her phone and loaded up the footage as they gathered around to watch. It had barely picked anything up apart from the noise. Charlotte and Elizabeth were difficult to make out but the slamming doors were very clear.

'Shit,' Adam said. 'Did anything else happen when you came back down?'

'No, Bella went straight off to sleep luckily and there was no other noise after all that. It just doesn't seem real. They've never acted like that before.'

Emma filled the kettle and got out three cups.

'I don't like that Bella's door was jammed shut. Was she okay?' Adam asked.

'She was fine. You saw in the video, she just said Charlotte was laughing. I don't think she'd hurt her. I don't think they'd hurt any of us. It just seems scary because it's the unknown. If there was an instruction manual for a haunted house we'd be fine.'

They all sat at the table for the next hour going over in detail what had happened the night before and the possible reasons for it. It had been the most activity they had experienced in the house in one night. Once more, they agreed the family must be trying to tell them something, but there was no way to talk with them directly.

Just after eight o'clock Catherine and Emma walked Bella to school. Bella said nothing about the night before. Even when Adam tried to ask her about it she just shrugged it off. She was still upset about her cake and didn't know what to say to her class, so Catherine told her she would speak to the teacher and some of the other mums outside to explain there had been an accident.

Adam said goodbye to Bella and waved them off down the path and decided on a shower. He had a quick look in each of the bedrooms to see if anything else had been knocked over in the night but all seemed okay. He undressed in the bedroom and grabbed his towel which had been left over the radiator. He felt like he was being watched, but he put it down to what he had been told of the night before and decided that he was making himself paranoid. After a quick shower, he dried himself off before getting dressed and making his way down to the kitchen to grab some breakfast. He had a couple of hours before he needed to set back off to work again.

Adam picked up his plate of toast and large cup of coffee and turned around to leave the kitchen. But there he was, standing in the doorway: the elderly and confused Henry. Something about him had changed. Adam had not actually seen him since their first day in the house when he had knocked on the door, but even then Henry had not looked him in the eye. He had just looked around, confused, playing with the buttons on his cardigan and repeating the same words. This time was different.

Henry stood in the doorway blocking Adam's way out of the kitchen. He stood up straight and looked at him directly in the eye. His hands were down by his side and his face was serious and determined.

'Find them,' he said.

Adam could not speak. He opened his mouth but his voice failed him. His feet felt glued to the floor and his hands were taken up with holding his drink and plate so he couldn't reach for his phone to open the camera. All he could do was stand and watch Henry, listening to his words.

'You must find them.' His voice was frail but no less demanding.

Henry then turned to walk away.

'Wait,' Adam could finally speak. He put his cup and plate back on the kitchen counter and walked after Henry who had now opened the front door. Adam stood back as Henry turned around to say his final words.

'Find them. Let us rest.' The door shut behind him. Adam was stunned. It took him a few seconds to realise what had just happened. He stepped forward and opened the door. Henry was nowhere to be seen but Adam could see Catherine and Emma walking back from the school. They waved, so he waved back but didn't stand by the door. He left it open for them and walked back into the kitchen trying to understand what had just happened.

'"Let us rest",' Catherine repeated once Adam had told her and Emma what had happened. 'Well, at least he spoke to you.'

'Would have been nice if he could stick around, though, to tell us *how* to let them rest,' Emma said.

'What do we take from that?' Adam asked. 'Are they here? Somewhere in the house and we need to find them?'

'But we can't find them until they make themselves known to us, like last night,' Catherine said.

'No, I mean the bodies. Their bodies must be here somewhere. All this "find them" business. Henry wants us to find them.'

'But Henry wouldn't accept that they had left him. He spent the rest of his life looking for them without success, so of course his spirit is going to tell us that. He had unfinished business and now he's wanting us to do the same.'

'Are you telling me you're still convinced that the family left him?' Adam asked Catherine. 'Or do you believe Henry's suspicions that something else happened? That they didn't leave him.'

'But… where do you think the bodies could be?' Emma asked.

'Here,' Adam said. 'In the house.'

CHAPTER 37

The rest of the week was uneventful. There were no more noises, no more disruptions and no more visits from Henry or any of the family. Emma was able to enjoy the next few days of her visit and all too soon it was Thursday and her last night. Adam and Catherine had decided to take her out for tea. They found a family-run restaurant in Skipton and enjoyed a wonderful evening of food, drink and sticky toffee pudding. When they were all feeling fat and bloated they made their way home. Bella was just about ready for bed.

'What the hell?' Adam said as he tried to walk through the front door. Something on the other side was blocking it. He finally pushed it open and found the cushions from the sofa in the hallway. They walked in and were stunned at what they saw. In the living room, there were books and DVDs all over the floor like they had been thrown from the shelves. In the kitchen, the drawers and cupboards had all been opened, papers had been strewn around the floor and one of the blinds had fallen from the window.

'Oh my God, call the police,' Catherine said, holding tightly on to Bella's hand.

'No, nothing's been taken. It was them,' Adam said.

'How can you tell?'

'Look.' He pointed at the back door. 'The chain is still on the door, so no one has come through there and the front door was locked. And they'd need to be able to fly to get through the conservatory at the moment with all the junk in there. No one has gotten in. It was our friends.'

'Is anything broken?' Emma asked.

'No, I don't think so.' Adam checked through all the cupboards and drawers before closing them. 'I don't even think that blind is broken; it's just come off on one side. I can sort that.'

'They're very messy, aren't they, Mummy?'

'Yes, Bella. I think they need to learn some manners, don't you? Why don't we go pick up the books and DVDs from the living room? Let's have a quick tidy up and then we can go to bed.'

Catherine and Bella headed off into the living room leaving Emma with Adam.

'Don't you think it's getting a bit too serious now? They're obviously disturbed. This is pretty extreme for a few "friendly" house ghosts.'

'Look, Emma, this isn't something we can just report to the authorities to come and fix. People still doubt the Enfield hauntings all these years later. I don't want people to be judging us in forty years' time for claiming to be in a haunted house.'

'But you *are* in a haunted house.'

'Yes, and there will be people out there who will call us liars. We can catch something on video and they'll still say it's fake. I don't want this to get in the papers and then Bella suffer for it in school. We can fix it, I'm sure of it.'

'If you say so. I'll pop the kettle on.'

'What time's your train tomorrow?'

'Not till eleven.'

CHAPTER 38

'Welcome home, flower,' Adam said as Bella walked through the door followed by Catherine. 'Did you have a fun night at Janey's?' He scooped her up for a cuddle.

'Yes, it was fun.'

'Oh yeah? What did you get up to?'

'We played and ate pizza and watched films.'

'And where is my pizza? Did you not bring me any home?'

'Ha-ha, no, we ate it all.'

'What, all of it? You greedy mares.' He tickled her as she was trapped in his grasp. She giggled and tried to fight against it.

'Janey's mum said she was very well behaved and very polite,' Catherine said.

'That's what I like to hear.' Adam put her down. 'Are you going to help me in the garden again today? We need to mow the lawn and pull up some weeds.'

'Can I go on my swings?'

'And shout orders at me from across the garden?' Bella nodded. 'I think that's a fair deal. Take your things upstairs and I'll meet you outside.'

Bella ran up the stairs with her overnight bag and into her

bedroom. She could tell straight away that Charlotte had been in her room again. When Bella had left it yesterday her bed had been nicely made, but now the blankets were ruffled like someone had sat there and the pillows had been knocked off. Barney had also been moved from the bed to her dressing table chair and her wardrobe was wide open with some clothes on the floor that had been pulled from the hangers. It didn't bother Bella. It always felt like a game.

When Bella was sorted, she made her way downstairs. Her mum was in the kitchen tidying up so she went straight out the back door and ran directly to the swings. She could see her dad in the shed pulling out his gardening tools as she began to swing higher and higher.

She didn't notice them at first, but when she saw their faces she felt she had to stop. There was something about their expressions that made her feel uneasy. Were they looking at her? Were they looking behind her? She couldn't tell.

Elizabeth was standing in the bedroom window with both her hands on the glass and she was mouthing some words, the same words over and over. Charlotte was in the middle of the kitchen facing the open door, unnoticed by Bella's mum, who was walking around her. There was another girl in the window of her mum's office who Bella had never seen before but instantly knew was Mary.

Catherine walked past the door and noticed Bella was not swinging or smiling but staring at the house. She couldn't imagine what could be so interesting. She put down the cloth in her hand and stepped outside, shielding her eyes from the sun.

'What's the matter, Bella?' she called across the garden. Bella didn't answer. Adam overheard and looked up from the lawnmower, which he had been cleaning by the shed. 'Bella?' Catherine reached her daughter who seemed to be completely zoned out. Adam left the lawnmower upside down on the ground and walked over to join them.

'What's up with her?' he asked.

'I don't know.' They both knelt down in front of her. 'Bella? What's the matter? What's wrong?'

Bella did not take her eyes from the house and she did not speak. She could not speak. She lifted her right hand and pointed at the house. Adam and Catherine turned and saw the figures in the house. They both stood up.

'What are they looking at?' Adam asked.

'You're okay, Bella. They can't hurt you. I think they're jealous of your swing, that's all.'

'No, they're staring behind the swings, at the ground,' Adam observed.

'Why?'

'That's where they are,' Bella suddenly said. Adam and Catherine both turned to look at her. 'That's what she's saying to us. They're in the ground.'

CHAPTER 39

July 1916

My dearest Elizabeth,

I am now en route to the hospital to see out my last few weeks here. I am looking forward to a bath and a change of clothes. I will not miss the cold nights in the trenches and being waist deep in water whilst helping the injured.

I will write again soon when I have arrived and settled properly.

Yours,

Henry.

My dearest Elizabeth,

I arrived a few days ago and already feel so much better in myself. I thought some of your letters would have been here waiting for me but they have possibly been sent to the wrong place. I cannot wait until I receive them. I always hold them close and close my eyes as I can almost smell you on the paper and I can imagine that we are together again. Not long now, my love.

I will write to the children tonight.
All my love,
Henry.

To Mary, Charlotte and Toby,

I cannot wait to see you all. You will be happy to know that I have obtained a box of those biscuits I told you about and have hidden them in my bag ready to bring home for you all to share. It has been hard not to eat them all myself!

I know you have been supporting Michael. He has had a difficult time lately. From what I hear he has made wonderful progress and I know I have you to thank for that. I am so proud of you all.

Write me some letters soon.

From your loving father.

My dearest wife,

There is a delivery coming in tomorrow from the Red Cross. There will be medical supplies and fresh, new uniforms for us. I do not see the point in having some myself as I will not be returning until September but they are insisting. I have heard that they are also bringing letters from England that were never delivered. I am confident that yours will be among them so I can read them tomorrow night.

I must go for now.

Yours,

Henry.

My dearest wife,

Your letters did not come with the Red Cross as I was expecting. I was so upset and disappointed. Hopefully they will come soon.

I have been working alongside Lt Armstrong from Long Preston, not far from you at home. He is an acquaintance of His Lordship's. I do not remember him; however, he remembers my father. He has been kind enough to tell me stories of my father when he was in service. How, over the years Lt Armstrong and His Lordship became close and then when I came along, how Her Ladyship took an instant shine to me as though I were her own.

I will never forget their kindness. If not for them then we may never have met. I will always be grateful.

Tomorrow, Lt Armstrong leaves the hospital to return to the front. I have told him that, after the war, he should visit us and meet my wonderful family. He said he would be delighted.

All my love,

Henry.

My dearest Elizabeth,

Your letters still have not arrived. The war office assures me that nothing has been sent to the wrong place. I am not sure what is going on.

I am now in my second week at the hospital and have been allowed a day off to rest. I find myself feeling very lost with nothing to do. I have read some of your past letters and noticed the last one is dated the start of June. I hope the reason I have not had anything since is just a problem with the mail delivery. Maybe you have not been receiving mine either and are equally as worried.

I have to admit, I am getting concerned.

Yours,

Henry.

My dearest Elizabeth,

Last night I dreamt of our wedding day. Every detail was so clear it was like I was back at the church with you, saying our vows. I remembered how I felt as I saw you enter the church and walk down the aisle towards me, with your mother's veil covering your face. My heart beat so fast when I saw you in your beautiful dress. The veil teased me, hiding your face, but I could almost see your smile as you got closer and closer, until eventually you were standing next to me.

That was the best day of my life. Then came the children, our wonderful children. I do hope we can have more someday, if God allows us.

I cannot stop thinking about you. I am worried about you and I think that is why I had the dream.

I am deeply concerned that it has been so long since I heard from you. I have one more week here and then I will be venturing back home to you. I might even get to you before this letter does.

Yours,

Henry.

To Elizabeth,

I cannot sleep with worry. I cannot understand why there have been no letters. The other men receive letters almost daily from their families. I presume that someone would write to tell me if something had happened to you, so I thank God that this has not occurred. I am sure Aunt Ruth would write to me if needs be.

The sergeant offered to have someone sent to the house to check, but by the time any report comes back I will be on my way home anyway.

I leave in two days. I will arrive at the train station on the 12th of August. Please be there. Please be at the station to meet me as we agreed. Please be there.

Your beloved husband,

Henry.

CHAPTER 40

July 2016

*I*t was the first day of the summer holidays. Catherine rolled over in bed and checked the time. It was half seven in the morning. Her body clock refused to let her sleep in, which she hated and she could have done with more rest due to the sleepless night they had had the night before. Adam was still asleep next to her, as was Bella on the blow-up bed on the floor. They'd decided that Bella would sleep in their room with them for the time being. The nights were varied. Some were peaceful and uneventful. Others though, like last night, were disruptive and scary. Bella was now fearful of what was happening in the house and no longer liked her frequent visits from Charlotte.

Catherine noticed that the bedroom door was open even though it had been closed when she'd finally drifted off to sleep. The curtains too had been pulled slightly open. She quietly sat up in bed and put her feet on the floor, careful not to touch Bella's temporary bed. She picked up her phone and started browsing

Facebook. Emma had posted photos of a launch party she had been to the night before. Adam stirred next to her.

'Are you all right?' he asked.

'Yes, can't sleep.' She put her phone down and looked back at him. He had his arm over his eyes blocking out the light coming from the bedroom window.

'Did you open those?' he asked, looking at the curtains.

'Nope. Must have been one of our friends.'

Adam yawned and stretched before rolling out of bed and putting on some shorts and a T-shirt. He walked around the bed and pointed at the open door.

'Same. One of our friends but I don't know which one.' Catherine noticed Bella move slightly and then open her eyes. 'Good morning, flower. Are you okay?'

'Yeah.'

'Did you sleep all right?' Adam asked.

'Elizabeth was in the room. I saw her looking outside as it was getting light. She didn't move away from the window but then I went to sleep.'

'So that's who opened the curtains then,' Catherine said. 'Are you hungry? Do you want some toast? I can bring it up for you if you want to say here.'

'Are you both going downstairs?' she asked.

'Yes, darling.'

'I'll come too.' Bella threw back her covers and got up. She did not need to think about it for long. She didn't want to be left upstairs on her own. 'Will you come to the bathroom with me, Mummy?'

'Course I will. Come on, we'll go now.'

Catherine held out her hand and she and Bella made their way to the bathroom as Adam headed downstairs to the kitchen. He had his phone in his hand checking his emails as he made his way down the stairs. There was the message he had been waiting for from Amazon:

Thank you for your recent order of a
Lightweight Metal Detector. Your item
will be delivered today.

Excellent, he thought. Now they would be able to crack on
with searching the garden and hopefully put an end to all this.
He opened the blinds. There were thick dark clouds in the sky
threatening a huge downpour. Nothing could delay it any
further; he had to start searching the garden today. It had taken a
lot of research to make sure he picked the right metal detector.
There were so many reviews to read through. Of course, none
said anything about using them to find bodies but there were
some positive reports about this particular design being good
for locating items hidden deep in the ground. He had to start
today.

Once Catherine and Bella joined him in the kitchen he made
a start on some breakfast.

'Can we go out today?' Bella asked with a mouthful of toast.

'Where do you want to go?' Catherine said.

'Anywhere. Let's go see Nanna and Granddad!'

'We're going down there at the weekend, Bella. We can't go
yet. It's only Monday. What else do you want to do?'

'Anything, I just want to go out.'

'Why do you want to go out so much?' Adam asked.

'Because...' she stuttered, looking at her plate, 'because, it's... I
don't like them anymore.'

'What don't you like? The ghosts?'

She nodded her head. 'They're angry all the time. They make
noise. I don't like them.'

Adam and Catherine looked at each other.

'Bella, darling, we're trying to help them now. They'll go away
soon. They don't mean to scare us; they're just very upset.'
Catherine squeezed her daughter's leg and smiled but Bella was
starting to get upset.

'But–' She sobbed. '–they try and scare me.' She wiped her eyes with her hands getting toast crumbs on her face.

'Oh, come here.' Catherine held out her arms and Bella clung on to her mum. Catherine looked up at Adam.

'Bella,' he said, 'why don't I give Nanna a call and see if you can go stay with her for the week? Then Mum and me can get on with helping our house guests and you don't need to worry. How about that?'

'Are you going to tell them what's been going on?' Catherine asked.

'I'll have to. You wait here, I'll give them a call.'

Adam went into the living room to call his parents. Now that Bella was upset and scared to be in the house they had to take action. If Bella was out of the house they could search the garden quicker. Had their circumstances been different they would have moved out there and then but, sadly, money was not that easy to come by. Their mortgage was manageable but it didn't leave enough to move somewhere else.

'What if Nanna is busy and I can't stay?' Bella asked, still in her mother's arms.

'I'm sure it'll be fine. She's only part time at Tesco, and Granddad is retired so it won't be a problem. We'll see what Daddy says when he gets back. Why don't we finish our breakfast and then we can get dressed?'

Bella moved back over to her chair to finish the rest of her toast and Catherine got up to make another drink for herself and Adam. After a few minutes, he walked back in.

'Well, that's sorted then, Bella. You'll be sleeping at Nanna's for the week. She said you can stay as long as necessary.'

'Great,' Catherine said. 'What time are we taking her?'

'Well, they're going to come here actually. I told my dad very briefly what has been happening. He just said they'll be here asap.'

'Let's go pack a bag!' Bella said excitedly, jumping off her chair.

'Hang on, hang on. There's no rush,' Catherine said. 'You can finish your breakfast and then we'll go get dressed and put some things together.'

~

'If that's your parents they must have been speeding down the motorway,' Catherine said as there was a knock on the door. Adam got up to answer it.

'It'll be Amazon. I had an email to say the metal detector will be delivered today.' He opened the door and signed for the large parcel that was handed to him by the postman. 'Thank you, pal. Bye.' He closed the door with his feet, needing both hands to carry the parcel, and took it straight to the kitchen, followed by Catherine and Bella, and placed it on the table.

'Woah.' Bella gasped as Adam pulled it from the box and held it out.

'And how the hell does it work?'

'Well–' Adam left the instructions in the box. '–I think it's just a case of charging this thing up–' He pulled out a battery pack wrapped in bubble wrap. '–then attaching it to this thing here–' He motioned to the section under the handle. '–then pressing this switch here–' He pointed to a switch by the handle. '–and then, Bob's your uncle.'

'I tell you what, you get it on charge and *I'll* read the instructions.' Catherine pulled out the instruction manual and started flicking through pages.

'What does it say?' he asked.

'Pretty much what you said but more technical. Just stick it on charge.'

'Can we take it outside now?' Bella asked, running to the door.

'Not yet, Bella. It needs a few hours to charge first. Oh–' The phone started to ring. 'I'll go get it.' She hurried back into the living room. 'Hello?'

'Hello, is that Catherine? It's Anne here from Dory's Corner.'

'Hello, Anne. It's good to hear from you.' It had been several weeks since they'd met up to speak about Anne's idea. They had worked out some plans and discussed a financial arrangement and Anne said she would get back in touch once a contract had been drawn up so it would be official.

'I'm sorry it's taken so long. We've been on holiday so decided to leave it until we got back. The contract is ready to be signed so I can bring it over sometime this week if you like? Or you could come down to the café and bring Bella? Whatever is easiest for you.'

'Well, Bella is going to my mother-in-law's shortly for a week or two and we have a lot going on here. Actually, I've got two wedding cakes to do this week...'

'I can pop over, it's no problem. I'll call round one evening once the shop has shut.'

'That'd be fab. I'll be in all week and Adam is off work now, so you'll definitely catch us.'

'Brilliant, I will see you soon.'

'Bye.'

Catherine had almost forgotten about the two wedding cakes for the weekend, which was hard to believe since the first one was for the biggest bridezilla Catherine had ever met. Her ideas kept changing and there were constant messages from her with new details to add. In the end, Catherine had had to put her foot down and tell her to leave it alone or she could have her deposit back and find someone else. It seemed to do the trick but Catherine was not expecting any kind of tip from her. She was secretly hoping the business with the café would be a success so she could limit the number of wedding cakes she had to do. She loved her work and the reactions from the couples when the cakes were delivered, but every now and then there was a nightmare of a bride who made things very difficult or wanted the cake to be discounted as much as possible.

CHAPTER 41

'They're here! They're here!' Bella shouted as she saw her Nanna and Granddad park up and walk down the garden path.

'Go on then, you can open the door,' Catherine said. She was in the kitchen so filled the kettle ready to make them all a drink. Catherine loved it when Anita and Dom came to the house. It was so different to when her own parents visited. There were no judgements or picky comments, just genuine and pleasant conversation.

Dom came into the kitchen carrying Bella, followed by Anita.

'We're so glad you could come out here.' Catherine walked towards them and Anita grabbed her for a big, motherly hug.

'Not a problem, not at all.' Anita pulled back. 'Oh, your hair is looking lovely, have you had it cut? It looks so healthy. Doesn't it look healthy, Dom?'

'Fabulous,' he said sarcastically as Catherine laughed.

'Thank you. No, it's not been cut; I changed my shampoo, so might be that.'

'You look wonderful. You always do.' Anita smiled. 'Where's Adam?'

'He's just outside. Bella why don't you go get your dad?' Dom put Bella down and she ran out the back door shouting for her dad.

'So, what's going on? Adam was very vague, but said you need to dig up the garden,' Dom said.

'Well, it's a long story. I'll wait until he's here to tell you. Would you like a cuppa?'

'We'd love one. Take off your coat, Dom. We won't be going back yet.'

'Are you off work, Anita?' Catherine asked.

'I am today. I'm in tomorrow and Wednesday and then I have a couple of weeks off for myself. We were debating going away somewhere but might have to put it off now.'

'Aw no, don't change your plans for us.'

'Don't be silly, Bella takes priority. And we can always take her with us if we do decide to go somewhere. It depends what you've got to tell us.'

'Hello!' Adam shouted from the garden. He ran up to the door and took off his boots. 'Sorry, I was just in the shed.' He stepped into the house and hugged his parents.

'It's all right, son, we're not in a rush.'

'Why don't you all go sit down in the living room? I'll bring the drinks and Adam can start to fill you in. Bella, you stay here and give me a hand, okay?'

Adam and his parents made their way into the living room and Catherine took her time with the drinks. She didn't want Bella to hear too much of it. After ten minutes, she put the drinks on a tray and joined them, placing the tray on the coffee table.

'So, that's what the metal detector is for then?' Dom asked.

'Yes, we're going to try to find them. They have to be out there.'

Adam's mum had gone very pale. Her wide eyes were watching her son speak as though waiting for him to laugh and say it was all a joke. The hand that had been covering her mouth moved down to her husband's leg. She looked to Catherine who sat down beside Adam.

'I don't know how you've managed to stay here for this long,' Anita said. 'I don't think I could cope. I don't feel right even now sitting in here.'

'To be honest it barely even seems real until we talk about it out loud,' Catherine said. 'It was fine until it started to bother Bella, which was only recently.'

'Well, Bella can stay with us as long as you need. There's no school so that's not a problem. We'll look after her, won't we, Dom?'

Dom had gone quiet. He was looking at his son and rubbing his chin as he thought about it. 'Look, Catherine has work to do herself. You can't do this on your own. Once your mum is finished with work I'll come over and help you with it. I'll sleep in the spare room. It doesn't bother me. I'll come up Thursday and help you get on with it.'

'Are you sure you can sleep here?' Anita asked him.

'It'll be fine. They can't hurt me. But Catherine can't put work off, and Adam will need an extra pair of hands for the digging and whatnot. I'll come back up Thursday morning.'

'Dad, that'd be great.'

'Yes, thank you. I have two cakes to do and I don't know when Anne will want her first cake for the shop.'

'That's settled then. Come on, Bella. Go get a bag packed. You'll be staying with us for a while.'

Bella looked at her mum.

'Do you want me to go upstairs with you?' she asked, knowing Bella would not want to be up there alone.

'Yes, please,' Bella said, shyly.

'I can go up with you, Bella,' Anita said. 'Come on, let's get packed.'

CHAPTER 42

*a*dam and Catherine had been awake for a while thanks to the loud footsteps on the landing through the night. They'd started at three o'clock, but every time Adam got out of bed to investigate they stopped again. Catherine made the point that it was a good thing they were in a detached house. If they'd had any neighbours, they would surely complain about the noise.

Eventually they gave up trying to sleep and went downstairs. Adam checked that the metal detector was fully charged whilst Catherine made them both some toast and a cup of coffee. She could spare the morning to help in the garden but needed to get started on the cakes that afternoon. She had left it late enough already.

'I hope the neighbours don't see us out there,' she said. 'It will look a bit odd being out at this time searching and digging up random patches.'

'If the neighbours care enough they can bloody well help us.' Adam was grumpy. It was barely eight o'clock.

'Here.' She handed him his coffee. 'Drink this.'

'Thanks, sorry. I just want this over with now.'

'I know, me too.' She smiled at him. 'Come on, show me how this thing works then, because I won't be the one digging.'

Once they had finished their breakfast and checked the machine was charged they headed outside. Adam had located the spade the day before and they were ready to begin their mission. Catherine put on the headset and Adam made sure she knew what sounds and alerts to listen out for. He wrapped his wedding ring in a handkerchief and buried it a few inches deep in the soil when Catherine wasn't looking and made her search for it. As soon as she found it they felt confident enough to begin.

Adam had drawn up a grid of the garden so they could keep track of where they had searched. They would start nearest the house where it would be easiest to dig if necessary as it was all lawn. The further down the garden they went the more stones and tree roots would get in their way.

After two hours, they had only done a small section but they didn't want to rush for fear of missing something. So far, though, the only thing they had successfully pulled from the ground was an old rusty trowel head.

When it reached eleven o'clock they decided to take a much-needed break. The sun was hidden behind the thick clouds but it was very humid. Catherine had to head in shortly to start baking.

'I'm gonna need a shower before I do any baking. I'm so sticky.'

'Yeah, you smell a bit too.'

Catherine shoved Adam playfully as they sat on the grass enjoying the gentle, cool breeze.

'Look,' Adam said, 'she's watching us.'

Catherine looked up and sure enough Elizabeth was in their bedroom window looking down at them. There was something different about her face. Catherine noticed that she was wearing a slight smile; she looked hopeful. It spurred them both to carry on.

'Come on,' Catherine said. 'I'll do one more hour with you before I go in.'

~

After they had some lunch, Catherine went up for a quick shower before beginning on the cakes. Although they were both wedding cakes they had very simple designs so would not take up too much of her time. Both were being collected Saturday morning so she was not worried about getting them delivered herself. It took her the rest of the afternoon but they were finally baked and left out to cool. Decorating could now wait.

Catherine stepped outside to check on Adam. She wasn't sure how much longer he wanted to stay out in the garden. The clouds had changed colour and were now black mixed with a threatening shade of purple.

'Looks like a storm is brewing,' she called over to him. He looked up at the sky.

'Dammit. What time is it?'

'It's just past five. No luck then?'

'Nah, not even a penny.' He pulled off the headset. 'Might need to call it a night.' He looked up to the window and saw Elizabeth. 'Sorry, love. I'll be back out tomorrow.'

Catherine heard a knock at the door.

'If that's Henry,' Adam called, 'tell him we're doing our best!'

Catherine walked back through the kitchen where the aroma of freshly baked cake filled the air. Even after all this time it was still one of her favourite smells.

'Anne, hello, I wasn't expecting you so soon, come on in.' She opened the door fully and ushered Anne into the kitchen.

'Thank you. Sorry, I've had a relatively quiet day so fancied a walk over. I hope it's okay.'

'It's fine, of course it's fine. I'm excited to get things started. Can I get you something to drink?'

'Just a cuppa tea would be nice. Weak and milky please, two sugars.'

Catherine started to make the drink as Anne noticed the state of the garden. The sporadic patches where the grass had been dug up did not make sense.

'Err, are you... making some changes out there?' Anne's eyes followed Adam as he carried the spade into the shed.

'Kind of, nothing fancy, just a few ideas. So, did you bring the contracts?' Catherine changed the subject.

'Oh yes, here.' Anne pulled a document from her bag. 'It has everything we talked about. It's nothing too jargon-y, just for your peace of mind really. I think we should try it out for a few months and see what the customers like and review it after. Is that okay?'

'Yeah, that sounds perfect,' said Catherine as Adam walked into the kitchen. 'I'm happy with that.'

'Happy about what?' he asked. 'Oh, hello, Anne. How you doing?'

'Hello, Adam. You've been busy out there today it seems.'

He looked at Catherine who handed Anne her cup of tea.

'I was telling Anne that we're trying a few things out in the garden, to make it look a bit nicer.'

'Oh, yes, well, we've left it too late now really. We'll do a few bits and then tackle it properly next year.'

'Where's Bella?' Anne asked.

'Oh, she's staying with my mother for a while. They might take her on holiday for a treat but no plans yet.'

Catherine quickly signed the contract as Anne looked at Adam suspiciously, like he was hiding something.

'Shall we go sit down in the living room?' Catherine asked Anne. 'We can plan the first cakes.'

'Yes, sounds lovely.'

They headed into the living room. Anne looked around her at the house, taking in every detail.

'You know, my grandma used to mention this house a lot when I was little. Her grandmother knew the family that lived here in those days and was always talking about them.'

'Oh?' They took a seat on the couch. 'Did she say anything particularly interesting? I'm really keen to learn the history of the place.'

'You know what, I can't remember. I was young when she died but I do remember her saying "Abberton House this…" and "Abberton House that…". I wish she was still around; I'd ask her about it. Apparently, her grandmother was a bit of a know-it-all. Knew everyone else's business. Nothing got past her.'

'What was her mother's name?'

'Alice. Alice Holmes. She lived next to the old post office.'

'Oh wow. I was showing my sister where that was the last time she visited. I wonder what your great-great-grandma could tell us about the family.'

CHAPTER 43

'That was Dad on the phone.' Adam walked back into the living room and sat down next to Catherine. 'He'll be over first thing. I just hope this storm backs off.'

The rain was coming down hard and every few minutes there was a rumble in the sky above. It had started overnight and looked set to continue through lunchtime.

'It's going to be too muddy tomorrow, don't you think?' Catherine asked.

'Muddy, yes, but it will loosen up the soil and make it easier to dig.'

'Was Bella okay? Did you speak to her?'

'No, but Dad said she was fine. My mum has taken her out shopping before she starts work later. Dad said she slept in really late yesterday. She must have needed it.'

'Aw, poor thing. We should have done something about this sooner.'

'We're doing something about it now and that's all that matters. Well, we will when this rain buggers off.' They both looked out the window as the rain battered against the glass. 'What are you going to do today, then?'

'I might as well finish those cakes. What are you going to do?'

'Not much I can do. Unless you fancy a roast for tea? I can nip out and get a joint of beef from the butchers.'

'That sounds like a really good plan. I'll finish this cuppa and I'll crack on with those cakes.'

~

Adam had cooked a full roast dinner, which was ready by the time Catherine had finished decorating the first cake. She had been so busy and distracted that she did not notice the smells coming from the kitchen. Adam had slow cooked the meat in rich beef gravy. The potatoes had been roasted in goose fat. The Yorkshire puddings had risen perfectly and the vegetables had just finished boiling. Catherine was hit by the delicious aromas as soon as she opened the door from her office to the kitchen.

'Oh my God, this smells amazing.' Her empty stomach instantly started to grumble.

'Come here.' Adam pulled her towards him and using his thumb he wiped some icing sugar from her cheek.

'Ha-ha, oops! I'll go sort myself out first. Won't be long.'

Catherine ran out the room and up the stairs into the bathroom. She washed her hands and face, ready to eat. As she stepped out onto the landing she heard a noise from Bella's bedroom. She knew what it was, or rather *who* it was, so decided to ignore it and just head straight for the stairs, but as she lifted her foot to go down the first step, she heard the voice again. It made her stop. She was sure she knew who it was, but she couldn't make out what it was saying.

'Help.' It wasn't crying out, it was speaking very quietly, barely audible.

Catherine wanted to shout for Adam to come upstairs but he wouldn't hear her over the sound of the oven and extractor fan.

She tiptoed slowly down the landing to Bella's room. The door was shut.

'Help,' the delicate voice said again.

Carefully, Catherine pushed down the handle. Her heart felt like it was beating in her head. The room was dark but there was enough light to see Charlotte. She was standing facing the window with her back to Catherine. It sounded like she was crying softly.

'Cha... Charlotte?' Catherine could only manage a whisper but it was enough to get Charlotte's attention. She turned around slowly. The dark room cast a shadow across her face. 'Charlotte, Bella isn't here. She'll be back soon.'

Charlotte did not speak. She slowly turned back around to face the window. Catherine decided to leave her alone, when something flew across the room at her. Bella's Peppa Pig alarm clock hit her arm, banging as it fell to the floor.

'Charlotte, please don't do that.'

Bella's wardrobe doors suddenly burst open and clothes started to fly out in Catherine's direction. They blocked her view of Charlotte as they came at her, one after another. Catherine was forced backwards out of the room and towards her own bedroom by the clothes. It was clear that Charlotte wanted her out. Catherine called for Adam as jumpers and T-shirts slapped her in the face. As she stepped further back and into her bedroom, batting away the clothes, she stumbled on a jumper which had wrapped itself around her feet and she fell backwards, hitting her head on her bedside table. She held her head in pain, feeling the warm gush of blood filling her hand. When she opened her eyes, her vision was blurred but she could see a figure standing over her. It was a man, but she could not see his face. As her vision began to clear she could almost make out his features. She had never seen him in the house before, but he was looking at her with sorrow. His presence made her feel very uneasy and suddenly her head began to spin.

'Catherine!' She heard Adam shouting from the landing. He ran into the bedroom and lifted her from the floor, noticing the blood in her hair and on the side of the bedside table. 'Catherine, don't go to sleep. Stay awake. Can you hear me? Don't close your eyes.'

By the time the ambulance crew left, Catherine was feeling better. The paramedics were satisfied that she did not have concussion and just needed to take it easy. The cut to the back of her head was only minor. She took some paracetamol for the pain and was finally able to eat her tea. Rather than sit up at the table, Adam brought it to her on a tray where she could sit in comfort in the living room.

'And you don't know who the man was?' Adam asked.

'No, his face wasn't that clear. It definitely wasn't Henry, but I don't know who it was. No one we've come across before. Did you hear me fall, then?'

'No, it was strange. There was a whisper in my ear. That's the only way I can describe it. I couldn't make out what it said, but… I knew I had to go see if you were okay. And then I saw the state of the landing and knew something was up. We should just leave Bella's room alone until all this is over. We don't need to go in there. Are you all right?'

'Yeah, just a bit shaken up by it. It didn't feel like I just accidentally fell and hit my head, though. I can't explain it. It felt like that was meant to happen. I was meant to fall and hit my head to see that man. I don't know. Never mind. Forget it. What time is your dad coming tomorrow?'

CHAPTER 44

*T*he rain continued until Friday morning. Adam's dad
arrived on Thursday morning but told them it would
be crazy to even think about digging in those conditions. It
would be a waste of fuel for him to drive home again so he stayed
over anyway. Friday afternoon was clear and the heat from the
sun seemed to do the trick.

'Right,' Dom said, 'it's forecast to be sunny all weekend. We'll
go out first thing in the morning.'

On Saturday morning, two grooms from two separate weddings
came to collect their cakes from Catherine, each accompanied by
their best men. The weddings were at nearby venues and it was
their jobs to make sure the venues were ready and decorated for
their brides. Catherine loved the handover. It was great seeing
the looks on people's faces when their cakes were unveiled to
them.

Adam and Dom were already outside checking the ground. It
was still very wet in the centre of the garden so they decided to

cover the edges for today to give it more chance to dry out properly.

Dom couldn't take his eyes off Elizabeth as she stood watching them in the bedroom window. It was the first time that he had seen a ghost.

'You know, if I didn't know any better I would've said that it was a real, live person stood up there,' he said.

'My sister thought so too, at Bella's party. She thought one of the guests had snuck up to have a snoop around,' Catherine said as she rubbed the back of her head. There was still a lump where she had hit it.

'Does that still hurt?' Adam asked.

'It just started to tingle as I looked up. It's fine. Do you want me to help?'

'No, you go sit down and put your feet up. Take it easy,' Dom said. 'We won't be able to do much anyway with the grass being this wet, but we'll do what we can.'

'Okay, give me a shout if you want anything.'

As the day wore on their search ended unsuccessfully. They did not find a thing. They were limited to where they could search due to the mud. And it was getting too messy.

'I'll just go home tonight and we'll have to pick it up again next weekend,' Dom said. 'Let it all dry out properly and we'll give it another go. Sorry, guys, but it's just impossible at the moment.'

'Do you want us to bring Bella back for now, then?' Catherine asked.

'That's up to you, but she's perfectly fine with us and, to be honest, Anita was so excited to have her stay over. She misses Bella not living so close by. It's made her really happy.'

'I know Bella misses you guys too. We didn't realise how lonely it could be out here.'

'Why don't you come stay with us for a few days? Have a break yourselves and come back next weekend with me. It's no bother, and your mum will love it.'

It did not take much convincing. Adam and Catherine had not realised it, but they needed a break from the house. They agreed that they would pack a bag that night and set off in the morning and return to their mission next weekend.

CHAPTER 45

August 1916

enry had butterflies in his tummy which were not helped by the train he was riding on. The carriage rattled as it heavily hit the tracks. He had been delayed coming out of London so was an hour later than planned, but he knew in his heart that Elizabeth would be waiting at the station for him like they had discussed. She had to be there.

He'd received her last letter back in June but he did not know when it had been written. The delay in postage meant it could have been written long before that. Henry kept all her letters in his shirt's chest pocket, so they were close to his heart.

Henry sat among other soldiers returning to their homes. They managed to laugh and joke with one another, excited to be reunited with their families, but Henry could not join in with their celebrations. He could not relax until he had his wife and children in his arms.

The train pulled into the station after what felt like an eternity of travelling. It was now late in the afternoon. The platform was full of women with their children waving at the carriages as they went by. Henry scouted the crowds from the window as the train slowed, passing everyone, looking for those four familiar faces, but he could not see them.

The train finally stopped with a hard jolt. Henry grabbed his bag down from the overhead storage but he decided to hang back for a while to allow the other soldiers to depart the train and meet their families and leave the station. That way, when he stepped out, there would not be as many people to search through for his own family.

They were not there. He checked everyone he could see but they were definitely not there. He suddenly heard a laugh. A cheeky child's laugh. His heart skipped a beat. It sounded so familiar; it had to be her.

'Charlotte?' he called out, looking behind him to where the sound came from. A child ran past him and into the arms of a soldier standing nearby. It was not Henry's daughter.

Henry decided not to hang around waiting for them and so he set off straight for the house, hoping that he would bump into them making their way down to the station, running late for a silly, forgivable reason.

He saw many familiar faces on his walk but no one stopped to speak to him. *Maybe they don't recognise me in uniform*, he thought as they glanced at him and hurried past. He didn't really care. He could speak to them and catch up another time. Right now, he just wanted to be home.

The house stood as it always had, and Henry started to feel emotional as soon as he saw it. He had been away for so long and he had worried that he would never return, as would be the case for so many of his fallen comrades.

He knocked on the door as he pushed it open. It wasn't locked, so they had to be in.

'Hello?' he called out. 'Where is everyone?' The house was

quiet. He walked into the living room where dust covered all the furniture. Elizabeth never let the house get dusty. It did not make sense. A foul smell was lingering, which he followed into the kitchen. On the table was a loaf of bread plagued with green and black mould. Henry had seen a lot of horrible things in France – amputation, injuries and rotten wounds – but the sight and smell of the mouldy bread made him retch.

Henry ran up the stairs and frantically in and out of all the bedrooms. The beds were made as they always were. He looked in all the wardrobes and drawers. All their clothes remained in place but the spare bedsheets were missing. A sudden and heavy feeling filled his stomach. Something that he prayed was not true. His family were missing but all their clothes remained in the house. They had evidently been gone for a while considering the state of the house, but some of the bedsheets had been taken. No, surely not...

'Oh my God.' He retched again, his stomach sick with fear. 'Where are they? Where are my family?'

CHAPTER 46

August 2016

*A*dam and Catherine returned from Adam's parents' house on the Friday night feeling relaxed and happy. Bella was back to her normal self and was more than happy to stay with her nanna for a little while longer. Dom would rejoin them on Sunday to continue helping them in the garden.

On Saturday morning, they woke up naturally a little after ten o'clock. Something they had not done in their own house for a while since all the activity had picked up. Their sleep had also been peaceful and undisturbed. Adam got up and out of bed.

'I think we should go back out today. What do you think?' He pulled back the curtains and stretched as he looked out into the garden.

'Don't you want to wait for your dad?' Adam did not respond. 'Adam? Adam?' Catherine sat up in bed, but Adam was focused on something in the garden.

'She looks down from here, doesn't she? This is where she

stands, right here in this spot, and she looks down there.' He pointed his finger, touching the glass. Catherine got out of bed to join him and see what he was talking about. 'There, look.' He was pointing down at Bella's play set.

'What about it?'

'There. That's where she was looking when Bella saw her speaking through the window. She wasn't looking directly at Bella, though, she was looking behind her.'

'What are you saying?'

'That's where we cleared all the dead and broken trees, do you remember? When the three of us were out there tidying things up. They hadn't been planted there, though, it was like they had been dumped there at some point and grown from there.' Catherine understood what he was saying immediately. 'Come on, we have to go out there, now.'

They were soon out in the garden, moving Bella's play set out of the way. It was tricky as it was so large and awkward. Taking care not to break it they slowly managed to move it to the other side of the garden where they had already searched with the metal detector.

Catherine put on the headset and Adam had the spade ready. They were both determined to find them. This had to be it. It just had to be.

She switched on the machine and slowly started navigating her way in a straight line, turning around carefully and going back in the other direction trying not to miss anywhere. It took an hour to cover the entire area but nothing was picked up.

'Maybe we were wrong,' she said. 'There wasn't even a slight beep anywhere.'

'It has to be the spot. Look.' He pointed at the window; Elizabeth was there and she was nodding her head. 'See? She's nodding. This is it.'

'You try it.' She handed Adam the headset. 'See if you can hear something I can't.'

Adam put on the headset and covered the same area that Catherine had. He hovered over certain sections thinking he could hear something, but they were false alarms. An hour later, he had not come across anything either.

'Dammit,' he said, frustrated, throwing the headset onto the floor.

'Don't forget, she might not have been wearing her wedding ring,' Catherine said. 'This machine would be useless for picking up anything that doesn't have any metal in it.'

Adam looked at her for a moment. 'You're right,' he said. 'You're right.' He picked up the spade and marked out a large rectangular area to dig, eight feet long and six feet wide. 'This is the section.'

'Look, we can wait for your dad,' Catherine said, looking at the size of it knowing it would take a while to dig it all up.

'No, it's still early. We've got all day. I'll do all the digging if I have to. I don't mind.'

And so, Adam began. He dug down one foot in the area that he had marked, coming across roots from trees which were long dead. Catherine helped to pull them out of the way. There were stones as big as cats that caused problems too and had to be hauled out. After a few hours, Adam and Catherine were filthy, but nothing could stop them now.

Elizabeth had been joined in the bedroom window by Mary and Charlotte. It was the first time that Adam and Catherine had seen the three of them together. Elizabeth stood behind her girls with her hands on their shoulders. The girls were close together like they were holding on to each other. It was quite a family portrait.

It was getting late, the sun now hiding behind the house.

Adam and Catherine were three feet down into the hole but there was still no sign of any remains. They were beginning to give up hope.

'What's that?' Catherine asked. Adam had not noticed. He was rubbing the sweat off his face with his muddy arm.

'What's what?' he asked.

'That, there, sticking out. What is it?' She pointed at the tip of something brown poking out of the ground. It wasn't a stone. It looked like the remains of cloth, stained from the soil.

Adam stepped back into the hole and pulled at the bit of material, revealing more as the soil around it loosened. He heaved out what could have been a shirt. A man's shirt. It was brown from the muck but also was covered in darker stains which resembled old, dried blood. He dropped it and carried on digging, soon revealing a horrific sight.

'Is... is that them?' Catherine asked, her voice shaking as the shapes began to appear.

'I don't know.' Adam rubbed his head. 'I'll dig around and see what else comes up.'

Adam very gently brushed soil back revealing more of the shapes in the ground, not wanting to cause any damage.

'Wait, hang on.' Catherine ran back to the shed and pulled out a broom and took it back to Adam. 'Use this.'

Adam began to brush over the shapes, eventually revealing not one, but four body-shaped bundles wrapped in sheets and placed on top of each other. The bundle on top was small, the size of a child younger than Bella.

'Oh my God.' Catherine covered her face. 'Oh my God.' She began to cry. 'That's a child. That's a baby. They're all there. Oh my God, Adam.'

Adam jumped out of the hole and held his wife close as she cried into his chest.

'It's okay, calm down, it's okay. We've done it. We've done it.' Adam looked up and the family were still in the window. They all held on to each other. The girls hugged each other and Elizabeth was suddenly carrying a small boy. She was holding him tightly, as though she had not seen him for a hundred years.

Adam was so distracted that it took him a moment to notice Henry.

'Cat, look, he's here.'

Catherine lifted her head from Adam's chest. Her eyes were red from crying. Henry stood by the back door, watching them, a grave look on his face.

He walked over slowly, peering into the trench that Adam had dug, revealing the terrible sight of his beloved family. He seemed to take in what he was seeing, and there were tears in his eyes.

'My family,' he said, nodding his head, accepting what was in front of him. He climbed down into the hole and put his hand on the head of one of the bodies and closed his eyes.

A noise behind Catherine and Adam startled them. They spun round but it was only the call of a pheasant. When they turned back around, Henry was gone. The family in the window had also disappeared.

'Is that it?' Catherine asked. 'Is it over?'

'I think it is.' It was silent all around them. For the first time in months they were not being watched. 'Come on.' Adam kissed Catherine on the side of her head. 'We'll need to call the police. They'll take them away and they'll finally be at peace.'

EPILOGUE

June 1916

'*A*re you really coming with me? Do you mean it?'

'Yes, I do.' Elizabeth smiled, not quite believing what she was doing. 'I love you, Michael.'

'I love you too.'

She turned and hurried up the stairs to her bedroom. Michael walked into the kitchen to make them both a drink. In his entire life, he had never felt so happy. They were finally leaving together. This was it.

He had never been to Scotland, but he knew he had a lot of family who lived up there. He had met some of them when he was younger when they had come to visit. There were a lot of cousins. After his mother died, they used to write to his dad to beg him to move up there with Michael, but his dad was a stubborn man and would not leave. Michael knew their names and had a rough idea of where they lived.

He boiled some water and prepared a tray with some tea, milk and sugar. He picked it up to take upstairs to Elizabeth where he would help her to pack and then go to bed with her.

Elizabeth pulled down a suitcase from the top of the wardrobe. There was another behind it, but she would need Michael to help get that one down as she could not reach it. She opened the wardrobe and began to select which clothes she would take with her. She would not need any of her nice dresses, just her loose fitting ones to allow for the baby growing in her belly. She could make new ones when she needed, but for now she had to pack light. Then she saw it: the box containing her wedding dress.

She had kept it safely wrapped in a blanket inside the box and left it in the back of the wardrobe, hoping one day it could be passed on to Mary. She knelt down to open the lid, pulled back the blanket and there it was, still perfectly white. The lace was faultless, even after all these years. The pearly white buttons were all still in place. Elizabeth was suddenly reminded of the day that she and Henry said their vows. She had now broken a major vow, she knew, but despite that she realised she could not make the children believe that their father was dead. Henry was a wonderful man and father. At that moment she knew deep down that she needed to stay with him, and at least give him the chance to decide what he wanted to do with her. She would spend the rest of her life making it up to him. He might never trust her again, but there was one thing she could do to ensure she would never betray him again. She would need to tell Michael to leave, alone. He would need to go to Scotland without her.

'I've brought you a drink.' Michael walked into the bedroom and saw Elizabeth sitting on the floor holding her wedding veil. 'Are you okay?'

'Michael, I can't do this. I've decided I'm staying.' Michael turned his back to her and put the tray on top of the chest of drawers at the back of the room. He kept his back to her. 'I've made up my mind. I love you, I do, but Henry is who I need to be with.' She clung to the veil. 'You need to go, though. You have to go to Scotland on your own. Or go anywhere, just stay away from us.'

'Why are you doing this to me?' he said, quietly. 'Don't you understand? You have to leave with me.' He turned to face her, no longer begging but telling her. 'We are leaving tomorrow. Pack a suitcase or don't. We are going and that is final.'

'No, we are not. You are leaving; I am staying. You need to go now.'

Michael moved quickly, taking her by surprise as he pulled her up by her arms so she was standing in front of him. He did not let go of her.

'Pack your bag. We are leaving tonight!'

'No, we are not. You are going.' She fought against him, trying to pull out of his grip, but he was too strong. 'Let go, you're hurting me. Michael!'

'No! We're going. Now pack or I am doing it for you. I won't ask you again.'

Michael held on to her tightly as she tried to break away. She kicked out and knocked his leg. The pain shot through him as his false leg fell off and he let go. Elizabeth staggered back, catching her legs in the veil, which had somehow become wrapped around them, and fell, hitting her head on the bedside table. She collapsed on the floor, motionless.

'Elizabeth?' Michael stood over her still body. She did not respond. He knelt down beside her and turned her over so he could see her face. Blood was pouring from above her left eye and her eyes were open. 'Elizabeth? Can you hear me?' He put his fingers to her neck to check her pulse. It was slow. 'Elizabeth?' Her eyes moved to look at him and then he felt her pulse stop.

'No, no, Elizabeth, come back to me. You need to come back.' He tried to shake her awake, but it did not work. She was dead. 'No, no, no!' he cried. 'No, I'm sorry, I shouldn't have got mad,

I'm so sorry.' He held her body and cried. He held her for a long time, not wanting to let her go.

Time passed without him noticing. Michael held on to her all night. He was disturbed from his trance by the light shining through the curtains as the sun came up. His eyes hurt from crying and his legs had gone stiff from sitting on the floor for so long. He looked at Elizabeth again. Her face was pale and her perfect hair was covered in dried blood.

'I'm sorry.' He kissed her forehead and then pulled his arms from under her, placing her on the floor. He turned to use the bed to pull himself up, then picked up his false leg and put it back in place. He looked down on Elizabeth one last time before he checked the time. It was four thirty. He began to wonder what he should do. He would hang for this, he knew. There would be no sympathy for him now. Even if he were given a life prison sentence, he would not survive inside a jail. He had to hide her. He needed to hide all evidence and then do as Elizabeth had said: leave for good on his own.

He suddenly remembered the children. They would be awake soon for school. He could not hide all the evidence before then, and Mary would certainly raise the alarm. He would not get far before the police caught him and took him away. He could not let that happen. He had to get rid of them. All of them. As much as it pained him to do so there was no other option. He did not want them to suffer though. There would be no pain for them. But he had to act quickly and quietly before one of them woke up.

He walked to the girls' bedroom across the hall. He could hear them breathing, still deep in sleep. He held a cushion in his hand.

After he had taken care of the girls he walked to Toby's bedroom. Tears were pouring down his face as the realisation of what he had just done began to sink in, but he had to carry on. He had to finish. He looked down on Toby who was curled up in the corner of his crib. He looked so perfect and angelic in his white nightgown. Michael held out the cushion…

~

Michael sat at the kitchen table. He held the cushion close to him and cried. He could still smell the children on it as his tears slowly soaked into it. He'd had a long day on his own in the house. Time to sit and think about what he had done. He had killed the love of his life who was carrying his child. It could have been a boy who they would have named after his father, or a girl who they would have named after Elizabeth. An innocent baby who would never, ever know life. And Toby. Toby who had put so much trust in Michael. His first proper word was Michael's name and everyone had been so proud of him. Michael remembered that day, and how the family had been so kind to welcome him into their lives. For the first time, he had been a part of something so wonderful. Now he was filled with regret. *Why did I ruin the best thing to happen to me? This is all my fault, and now I need to hide the mess that I have made.* Michael knew he had very few options. He decided the best thing to do would be to bury the family together.

The sun was starting to go down so it would be safe to go to the back garden and dig a hole big enough for them all to be together. He had wrapped the bodies up in white bedsheets and cleaned the bedroom of all the blood before remaking the beds. He'd washed the blood from his hands and found some different clothes to wear. His blood-stained shirt would be buried along with the bodies.

He finished his cold cup of tea and went out to the shed to fetch a spade. It was a clear sky and the moon provided the light he needed to see what he was doing. He found a good spot in the middle of the garden where he knew he would not be troubled by tree roots and rocks. He dug deep into the soft soil and did not stop until he was a few feet down. It would not be long before the sun came up again, so he had to be quick. He went in through the back door of the house to where he had brought down the bodies.

He carried Elizabeth out first and laid her in the bottom of the grave. He then put Mary down beside her. Charlotte was placed on top of Mary and then Toby was placed on top of Elizabeth. He took off his muddied clothes and threw them in along with his blood-stained shirt. He picked up the spade and shovelled as much soil as he could on top of them, pressing it down firmly. Then he brought over some old tree branches and lay them on top to disguise where the grass was now missing. He put the spade back in the shed and looked over the garden as the sun began to rise.

Michael went back into the house to wash himself. He found some clean clothes of Henry's and left, heading for the river, where he would not be returning from.

THE END

A NOTE FROM THE PUBLISHER

Thank you for reading this book. If you enjoyed it please do consider leaving a review on Amazon to help others find it too.

We hate typos. All of our books have been rigorously edited and proofread, but sometimes mistakes do slip through. If you have spotted a typo, please do let us know and we can get it amended within hours.

info@bloodhoundbooks.com

Made in the USA
Las Vegas, NV
06 September 2022

54621237R10146